"You are dying to jump into bed with me . . ." Juan said.

He stopped the car and looked down at her, his dark eyes sparkling with reflected moonlight. "No man has ever touched you the way I have."

As if to illustrate his point, he ran his long fingers sensuously down her neck. She felt the searing warmth of his lips on hers and the melting turmoil of her resolve to resist him. Unable to hold back any longer, she encircled his strong neck with her arms as he devoured her mouth hungrily and the dark Cordovan night swirled mysteriously around them . . .

Second Chance at Love™

SUSANNA COLLINS

FLAMENCO NIGHTS

A JOVE BOOK

First Jove edition published June 1981

First printing

"Second Chance at Love" and the butterfly emblem are trademarks
belonging to Jove Publications, Inc.

Printed in the United States of America

Jove books are published by Jove Publications, Inc.,
200 Madison Avenue, New York, NY 10016

Chapter One

"YOU MUSTN'T HOLD anything against Chip. He was your best friend for too many years!" Rosie threw back her long, honey-colored hair and tried to concentrate on Francisco Goya's famous portrait of his mistress, *The Naked Maja*. She was annoyed at her brother Danny for bringing up the subject of Chip and her broken engagement when she wanted badly to forget it and immerse herself in the wonders of the Prado Museum in Madrid.

But even more disturbing than Danny's comments about Chip was the tall, dark-haired man who seemed to be shadowing them. Had he not been dressed in modern clothes, thought Rosie, he might have stepped down from an El Greco painting with his swarthy skin, high cheekbones and dark, deep-set eyes of a Spanish grandee. With her artistic perception, Rosie had quickly memorized every detail of the man including the casual, rich dark brown suede sports jacket and the rust-colored silk shirt open at the neck. The soft textures of the materials only accentuated the lean hardness of his body, the firm, decisive line of his jaw.

"I can't forgive Chip for walking out on you one week before the wedding," Danny continued.

"Chip was only looking out for himself," she sighed indifferently, hoping to dismiss the subject.

"Obviously," answered Danny bitterly.

"Oh Danny, imagine if we had gotten married. He would have gone after his freedom later, maybe even after we'd had a couple of kids. Everyone has a right to design his own life. Chip wanted to be free of responsibilities, to travel and see the world. And maybe that's not such a bad idea."

1

Rosie lifted her chin and shook out her long hair in a gesture that meant she was not going to let the bitterness of unrequited love and a broken engagement defeat her.

Once again, she was aware of the compelling dark eyes of the stranger who seemed more interested in her than in *The Naked Maja*. She knew he was standing too far away to have heard what she said, and yet she had the eerie feeling that he knew.

"Rosie, I am the one person who knows you well enough not to be fooled by all that nonchalance," said Danny, throwing a brotherly arm around her shoulder. "I know you're hurting. That's why I wanted you to come here. Spain has always been your real love. Now it's the place to start afresh.

"All your life you've had only one boyfriend. And I don't think Chip, though he was a good buddy of mine, ever really appreciated you. You're a beautiful girl, Rosie, an extraordinary beauty. But because Chip took you for granted, you have always taken yourself for granted. Here in Spain, the men won't let you forget that you're special. I've seen the heads spin around as we walk down the street. Even now, while we're talking, just look at the way that man is staring at you."

Rosie did not need to turn and look to know who her brother meant, but she found herself looking up anyway, catching the smoldering gaze of the handsome stranger's dark eyes. She blushed crimson and tried to pretend renewed interest in the painting, but the sensuous *Maja*'s direct gaze only increased her embarrassment and she escaped quickly down the hall to confront a staid Velázquez portrait of Felipe IV.

Danny was amused by his sister's reaction. "You see?? Flash those bright green eyes of yours and you'll have every *caballero* in Castile crawling to you on his hands and knees."

That man would never crawl an inch for any woman, she thought. She was shaken by his gaze, the sheer, blatant audacity of what could be read into it and wished her brother had taken offense rather than brushed it off lightly.

Inadvertently she stole another glance at the man, and to her surprise, he seemed to be waiting for it. He lowered his eyes slowly, taking in her shapely figure, then flashed her a smile. She realized that he expected her to respond to him in some way. Her heart was pounding irrationally as she turned back to Danny for support. "That man, he's so . . . so . . ."

"He appreciates beauty when he sees it. Why else would he be wandering around a place like this? Oh, don't get offended, Rosie. European men, especially Spaniards, are like that. It's a compliment."

Compliment or not, she refused to encourage him with another glance. No matter how common it might be in Europe, she would not be treated like a painting—an art object. To show him she was definitely not interested, she stared so hard at the Velázquez she thought she'd bored a hole into it.

He gazed at her another few seconds, then as though he'd had enough of an interesting work of art, moved on.

Rosie noted the way he walked. It was not quite a swagger, but the long-legged stride of an aristocrat. He was a man who was used to getting what he wanted from life. And that included women.

For the rest of the afternoon, Rosie found herself thinking about the handsome stranger. In so many of the paintings she saw his face, the compelling dark eyes, the tall, lean carriage and the haughty pride of a Spanish aristocrat.

Then she became angry with herself for allowing him to intrude on her appreciation of the great works of art she had waited a lifetime to see. It was hard enough to concentrate on them with Danny either reminding her of Chip or standing beside her, tense from boredom.

At one point she tried to interest him in the history and literature of the era. "It was a romantic time, Danny, when Lope de Vega wrote of love—a subject he knew better than anyone. Danny, you're not even listening to me!"

He smiled sheepishly, his pale blue eyes twinkling with mirth. With the untamed shock of golden hair falling over his forehead, he looked, Rosie decided, more like a naughty schoolboy. But he was twenty-five, a year older than she.

"It's just so ironic, Rosie. You were the one who gobbled up everything to do with Spain. I can't pretend to be interested in all this cultural stuff, and yet I'm the one who ended up living here."

"All the more reason you should learn something about it," she chided him gently. No one was ever able to get angry at Danny. His irresistible boyish grin and good nature usually dispelled any potential adversary. And yet he had always gone to battle for Rosie. She remembered the afternoon he marched home from the first grade proudly displaying a black eye he had acquired while defending her from a bully's taunt of "kindergarten baby."

Danny had been terribly upset about Chip's actions, and Rosie was secretly glad her brother had been in Spain when it erupted. Though she would have been grateful for the moral support, she feared what he might have done to Chip, despite their longstanding friendship.

"All I have to know about Spanish art is my wife, Rafaela," he laughed. "She's a masterpiece. And next to her, the town of Cordoba. Wait until you've seen that town, Rosie. It will make all this Prado stuff look amateurish."

Rosie promised herself that she would return to Madrid and the Prado Museum on her own after visiting Danny's home in Cordoba. There was too much to absorb in one quick walk through—and so many distractions. All the artists she admired most in the world were represented here, especially Velázquez and Goya.

She could find no rational explanation for her consuming fascination with Spain. There had been no Spanish ancestors in the Powell family tree, no inspiring high school Spanish teachers. But her enchantment had been part of her for as long as she could remember. And like the Spanish paintings and the enigmatic eyes of the handsome stranger, the concept of Spain touched her deeply.

She watched her brother Danny out of the corner of her eye. The rambling six foot ex-rodeo star who looked and felt so out of place in an art museum—had he been listening to her childish dreams of castles in Spain more closely than he had let on? How was it that on a summer trip to Europe, he'd fallen madly in love and married a beautiful Andalusian girl, a girl he barely knew. The whole family had been surprised.

It was not like Danny to fall quickly in love. He had always played the field with girls, refusing to tie himself down to only one. How had Rafaela managed to capture his heart so completely?

Rosie was selfishly glad that his wife Rafaela had not been able to leave her mother's restaurant in Cordoba to meet her plane in Madrid. It was not that Rosie disliked Danny's wife—they had gotten along wonderfully well when Danny brought her home to meet the family in Wichita—but she appreciated having Danny to herself for a few days.

They were standing in a small room looking at a large, violent painting by Goya. Rosie felt her throat go dry with emotion. Goya's work always affected her that way—even seeing reproductions in books. The paintings touched a nerve that almost frightened her. And now being close enough to see and touch the actual brush strokes was overwhelming.

She suddenly turned around just in time to catch another glimpse of the man who had caused her so much distress before. But it was a different look this time that they exchanged. Without expressing it in words, she knew that he felt the same emotional turbulence about the painting that she did. There was a silent understanding. He nodded, smiled, then disappeared into the corridor, leaving her feeling as shaken as before.

This time she had a mad urge to run down the hall after him. Instead, she turned to her brother. "How do you like this painting?"

"Wow! I can't believe this guy Goya painted an execution, just like he was there. I mean, this was before photography. You've got to admire something like this, even if you don't really understand it. I remember this painting from when Chip and I were here last summer . . ."

Danny's voice faded away as he caught the look on his sister's face. "I'm sorry. I keep bringing up Chip and I know it's hard for you."

"You can't stop talking about him just to spare my feelings."

"I don't know, Rosie. I want you to get over him, so I think that if I get you to talk, you'll feel better. But then you get that look on your face—that crushed, defeated look and I could kick myself for bringing it all back to you."

Oddly, Rosie realized that she was much more haunted by the memory of the insolent, handsome Spaniard and their silent encounters. She could not chase him from her thoughts. His vibrant image pursued her into dinner, and she found herself plunging into a discussion of Chip just to take her mind off the dark stranger.

"Funny, isn't it," she began more easily than she suspected she could, "how that trip to Europe you and Chip took last summer would affect each of you in a different way. You fell madly in love and married the girl of your dreams in Cordoba, and Chip decided not to settle down at all."

"I was bewitched," said Danny. "Maybe you will be too while you're here. I just hope to heaven it's in Cordoba. Then you can live close to me and Rafaela, and our kids will have cousins, and . . ."

"Danny," her mouth fell open in surprise. "I thought you and Rafaela planned to come back to Kansas. This sounds like you mean to stay in Spain forever."

"Calm down a minute, babe."

"Calm down?? When I might not ever see you again?" She hadn't meant to get so emotional, but the thought of doing without her brother had touched her more deeply than she realized.

"Wait 'til you see Cordoba," he said softly, his blue eyes very far away. "There's something, well, I'm not very good with words, but . . . it's *home*, Rosie."

"Your home is Wichita."

"Sure, I know. I was born and bred in the good old American Midwest; apple pie and ice cream, rodeos and football games. And I miss all that sometimes, Rosie. But Cordoba, with the white houses, the old horse-drawn buggies, the fresh smell of jasmine blossoms at night. And Rafaela." He said her name with a hushed reverence that reminded Rosie how much in love he was. She had never seen her brother so intensely serious or blissfully happy. Perhaps Spaniards did have a bewitching effect on people.

"But what about the rest of the family? We'll *all* miss you, not just me."

"My mother-in-law's restaurant does very well. Even better since I've been helping out. We plan to go back to Kansas at least once a year. That's more than Joey does since he moved to Atlanta three years ago."

"Well, you're happy and in love. That's all that matters," said Rosie on a positive note, though she was still not resigned to losing her favorite brother and best friend. She was suddenly resentful of Spain and its allure. And without warning, the dark man from the Prado popped into her mind again.

As they drove along the highway to Cordoba a few days later, she discovered that the vivid image of the stranger was impossible to dispel. Looking up at the stately fortress-castles on the hills, she imagined her lean *caballero* clad in shining armor, racing across the dusty brown hills on a black stallion alongside El Cid.

They stopped for lunch at a quaint roadside inn, recommended in the *Michelin Guide*. Excusing herself to wash her hands, Rosie left Danny in charge of ordering. When she returned to their table, her heart began to pound uncontrollably and she felt her face flush scarlet.

There was no mistaking him. It was the man from the Prado, seated at their table, chatting amiably with her brother.

The man stood up politely when Rosie arrived and held her hand. "*Encantado,*" he smiled slightly while his eyes travelled across her body in a quick appraisal reminiscent of the one in the Prado that made her knees feel like jelly.

"Rosie, you won't believe this," said Danny enthusiastically. "This is the guy we saw in the museum the other day. Remember, the one I told you was...," he stopped as he realized it probably wasn't right to acknowledge that blatant scrutiny of his sister.

"Oh, yes, I vaguely remember," she said nervously mustering an air of indifference.

The man showed a glimmer of strong white teeth between lips that tried to keep back a smile. *He* knew she remembered very well. "I hope I did not embarrass you," he said smoothly, "I was just apologizing to your brother for my rude stare. I thought he might have been your husband. But one does not see a woman of such exquisite beauty often, who stands out even when surrounded by so many other beautiful works of art."

There was an edge of mockery in his voice. Rosie knew he could not possibly mean the flowery words he said, and she glanced at Danny to see if he detected it. But he only seemed pleased that this man so eloquently appreciated his sister's undeniable charms.

"What a coincidence, Rosie," Danny continued, "Señor Arévalo lives in Cordoba and he's headed there right now! Oh, I forgot to introduce you. My sister, Rosie Powell, this is Juan de Arévalo."

Rosie's bright green eyes suddenly opened with new interest. "You're not Juan de Arévalo, the flamenco guitarist, are you?" She had four of his records, and now that she looked closely at him, he did resemble the photographs on the album covers.

"Guilty," he smiled. Rosie hoped to detect a glimmer of humility, but he was a virtuoso utterly lacking in that quality. One of the best classical-flamenco musicians in the world, he was obviously a man who considered his fame well deserved.

Instead of overwhelming her, this new knowledge had the opposite effect on Rosie. It put her at ease for it explained her bewildering fascination with him. Of course, she had recognized him from the album covers. That was all there was to it. Her preoccupation with him was nothing more than a subconscious attempt to place him. But recently she had seen his photograph somewhere else.

"You were in a national magazine recently," she said.

He shrugged with the indifference of a man whose face appeared in many publications.

"In New York. At one of those jet-setter discos," she continued.

"It is possible. I was in New York for a concert last month with the Philharmonic."

"Ah! Now I know why I remember!" she said triumphantly. "The actress Jane Sidney was with you. It was written up as the big romance of the century."

His mouth twisted into an amused grin. "One must be careful not to believe everything that is printed."

"How long have you lived in Cordoba?" asked Danny to bring the subject back to a plane of familiarity.

"All my life. And I'm anxious to return. It has been over a year. Too long to stay away from Cordoba." Rosie decided it might be the first sincere comment she'd heard him utter.

"I know what you mean," said Danny. "I was just telling Rosie how that town grows on you. I've only been away a few days and already I miss it."

"He misses his wife," she added playfully. "They've only been married six months."

Danny's face reddened with embarrassment. "Say, Juan, when you're in Cordoba, you'll have to stop by and say hello," he rallied back to change the subject. "My wife's mother owns what most people say is the best restaurant in Cordoba, the Conejo Blanco. It's not far from the mosque. You can't miss it. Everyone knows where it is."

Juan de Arévalo's muscles tightened about his narrow face and his dark eyes widened for a brief second. There was something dangerous beneath the surface of his taut skin, ready to explode. "Yes, I know the restaurant very well," he said with a hint of anger. "The food is excellent."

"Good, then it's settled. You must come by the first chance you get and I'll buy you a drink," said Danny. He had also noticed the change in Arévalo and wasn't sure how to continue.

"Yes," Juan responded coldly and abruptly stood up. "My pleasure to meet you both."

Danny shrugged as they watched him leave. "Weird guy. One minute he's all smiles and the next minute he bolts away like we insulted him. Who can figure?"

Rosie watched the Spaniard as he strode out the door, the well-tailored pants clinging to the hard muscles of his long legs, his suede jacket slung carelessly over his shoulder.

"Thank heavens you've never had an artistic temperament, Rosie," her brother shook his head.

Nothing Danny or the guidebooks had said about Cordoba could have prepared Rosie for the impact it had on her. She had been awed by the grandeur of Madrid, intrigued by the cold grey starkness of Toledo that echoed the somber El Greco paintings. But Cordoba was like rays of warm sunshine rushing through the fleecy white clouds on a summer day, a wash of pink watercolor brushed lightly across the golden brown buildings, spilling onto the red tiled rooftops and whitewashed houses.

Danny circled around the city so that she could arrive across the old Roman bridge that spanned the Guadalquivir River. "Best first view of the city is from here," he told her and pointed out the Alcazar, castle of the Christian Kings, on the left, and the Great Mosque straight ahead.

Rosie's history quickly came back to her: Cordoba, capital of the Roman Empire in Spain; Cordoba, caliphate under Moorish Spain, and Cordoba, center of assault against the Moors during Fernando and Isabel's war of reconquest.

It was in Cordoba that a Jewish poet of the twelfth century had written some of the most beautiful love poetry of all time, Cordoba where a love-struck caliph had built a luxurious palace for his favorite mistress, and where Christopher Columbus fell passionately in love with the beguiling Beatriz de Bobadilla.

As they drove through the narrow, winding streets, Rosie's heart danced in delight at the profusion of flowers, blooming in every size and color, spilling over like waterfalls from wrought iron balconies. Red carnations burst out of blue ceramic pots, white jasmine and hot pink bougain-

villea climbed over graceful Moorish arches. Rosie vowed
she had never seen so many flowers in so many colors. It
was as though a mad artist had gone crazy with his paints,
splattering colors at wild random over a white canvas. The
effect was intoxicating.

"I'll take you for a walk along the *callejas*, the narrow
alleyways you can't reach by car," promised Danny. "I've
seen hundreds of places for you to paint since I've been
here."

"I've already seen a thousand in just a few minutes," she
said breathlessly. "All these flowers in vivid colors; you
can barely see the walls of the houses!"

"Wait 'til you see inside them—the fountains and patios."

"Oh, Danny," she sighed, "No wonder you fell in love
in Cordoba. This is the most beautiful place I've ever seen
in my life!"

He stopped the car in front of a tiny, whitewashed house
with a red tiled roof covered with cobalt blue ceramic pots
overflowing with pink geraniums. A small woodcarved sign
announced that they were at the Conejo Blanco—the White
Rabbit.

Danny pushed open the intricately designed black
wrought iron gate, and they entered a charming tiny patio
with inlaid pebbles that created a floor pattern. A small
fountain in the center, with an ancient sculptured rabbit on
top, was lined around the edge with more of the blue potted
flowers. A half-dozen tables were under the shade of an
arcade, neatly set with red tablecloths. A few late luncheon
guests were still lingering over their coffee and looked up
to smile and wave at Danny carrying Rosie's luggage. He
put down the luggage, took Rosie by the hand and proudly
introduced his sister "Rosita" to the regular guests.

They passed through the whitewashed dining room with
a small bar at one end and another two dozen tables all set
with red tableclothes. There were copper pots and pans
decorating the walls, a wood hewn beamed ceiling, candles
on the tables, a blue ceramic tiled fireplace in the corner.
It had a cheerful, homey look.

Rafaela and her mother were busy in the kitchen, preparing for the dinner guests. They both dropped what they were doing and ran to kiss Rosie and Danny. Rosie's comprehension of Spanish escaped her for the moment, but it was not hard to gather that she was welcome from the emotional tears, smiles and hugs.

Seeing his sister's bewilderment, Danny quickly translated, "Rafaela says that she's so happy you arrived because she is an only child and has always wanted a sister, and her mother says that she has always wanted another daughter."

"Ah, we must speak English for our Rosa," commanded Señora Gómez.

"But I must learn Spanish," protested Rosie. "I'll catch on. I studied for four years in high school."

"It's true," said Danny. "She'll never learn the language if we all speak English."

"We compromise," announced Rafaela brightly. "For the first week, we speak English, then poom! nothing but Spanish!"

Señora Gómez showed Rosie upstairs to the living quarters of the house. "Danny says that in the U.S., not many people live above their restaurants or businesses like here, but I cannot understand that. For me, the restaurant is an extension of my own house. My guests are the guests in my own home. I cook for them like family."

The living room was a large, comfortable room of pastel colors with windows looking out into the street. The walls were covered with photographs of family, mostly of Rafaela in various stages of growing up. There were two huge wedding pictures of Danny and Rafaela, Señora Gómez beaming at their side.

Rosie was surprised to see a color photo of her entire family standing outside their Wichita farmhouse. "You see? Your family is in here, too. Danny has told us about each one of his brothers and sisters. I already know all their names. But you, he talks about the most."

Down a narrow hallway, also lined with photographs, Señora Gómez pointed out Danny's and Rafaela's room. There was a large Spanish bed, some religious paintings, and a huge framed Kansas State Fair Rodeo poster on one wall. Perhaps Danny missed Kansas more than he was willing to admit.

There was a smaller room at the end of the hall that the Señora indicated would be hers during her stay. It was a sunny, soft yellow room with peach-colored geraniums in the windows and posters of Spanish castles on the walls.

Señora Gómez pointed to the posters. "Rafaela wanted to make you feel at home, so she asked Danny how is your room in Kansas. And he told her you always have posters of Spanish castles. So all week, Rafaela is looking in Cordoba for posters of Spanish castles, and finally she found these in a travel agency near the Melia Hotel."

On the nightstand was an arrangement of tiny yellow tea roses with a delicate pink ribbon around the vase. A card beside it read, "For our own beautiful Rosa—Welcome to Cordoba."

In the corner, leaning against the wall, was a wooden easel. "Danny made that for you. He said your own would be too big to pack." Tears came to Rosie's eyes as she thought of the trouble they had all gone to, to make her welcome.

"We want so much for you to be happy here with us. Danny has told us so much about you and your paintings. I shall show you places to paint that tourists never see. And while you are here, you must become a *conquistadora*, make a conquest of a handsome Cordovan man. She pounded on her heart dramatically and winked, "I think Rafaela already has some bachelors picked out for you."

It was not difficult to imagine Señora Gómez as a young woman. There was still much youth in her plump, but handsome features. Rosie decided that she must have looked very much like Rafaela did now. They both had an infectious smile that brightened the space that surrounded them, twinkling bright eyes and a natural grace.

Rosie suddenly remembered the mysterious dark man they'd seen in the Prado and decided to tell Señora Gómez. Perhaps she could shed some light on his bizarre behavior. But as soon as she mentioned Juan de Arévalo's name, she saw a pained expression cross the Señora's normally cheerful face.

She placed a warning hand on Rosie's shoulder. "I know this Juan de Arévalo," she said in a low voice. "He has been away from Cordoba for a long time. Do not tell Rafaela that you met him."

"But why?"

"And you must tell your brother not to mention him either," she added.

Rosie was now totally confused. "Arévalo did seem a little strange, but . . ."

"It is a difficult story, Rosa." The Señora reflected a profound sadness from the depths of her soft brown eyes. But as quickly as the sadness has descended, it lifted like a passing storm cloud. "Now you must rest from your long, dusty trip. I will show you where is the bath and tonight, before the restaurant opens, we will open a bottle of our best sherry to celebrate your arrival." She gave Rosie a motherly hug. "So pretty a girl you are. ¡Madre de Dios! You will be the most popular girl in Cordoba with those green eyes and blond hair!"

Trying to heed the Señora's advice, Rosie waited to catch Danny alone to warn him about Juan de Arévalo, but he was busy the entire afternoon preparing for the evening guests. And by the time the people began trickling in after seven, he was fixing drinks at the bar.

They had all insisted that Rosie act like a guest, at least the first night. She had wanted to help wait on tables for she'd had experience in Wichita while putting herself through art school. But Danny suggested she wait until she was more proficient in the language. The Conejo Blanco was not a tourist restaurant; it catered to an established clientele, many of whom had been coming there since it opened fifteen years before. Rosie saw how Rafaela and her mother spoke to each one of the guests, greeting them as though they were family. A genuine feeling of warmth emanated from them and filled the restaurant, and Rosie decided that good food would always taste even more delicious in such a friendly atmosphere.

As she watched Rafaela flit between the tables like a butterfly, Rosie's admiration for her sister-in-law grew by the minute. She drew mental sketches of her, thinking she would surprise her with a portrait drawn from memory. Rosie had discovered she possessed a unique talent, being able to recreate scenes and people she had seen. It was like a photographic memory. She had realized she had it after reading how Francisco Goya did a sketch of his future mistress, the Duquesa de Alba, after only seeing her once.

Rafaela would be an easy subject with her sleek black hair swept down over her ears, the short straight nose, the black eyebrows arched over delicately large almond shaped eyes fringed with long black lashes. As Rosie watched her, she thought the expressions she'd most like to catch were in the fleeting moments she and Danny exchanged glances. There was a doelike expression in her eyes, wide with innocence and wonderment, as though every word from his lips were a precious jewel.

With all the girlfriends Danny had brought home, not one ever looked at him with such blind, adoring love. And never had she seen her brother so charmingly bewitched. There was scarcely a moment, even working behind the bar, that he didn't look up and smile at his wife.

Rosie felt almost a pang of envy watching them, thinking about her own broken engagement. But she and Chip had never been so wrapped up in each other. Their relationship had always been familiar and comfortable, and now that she thought about it, deadly dull. But it had been love, at least on her part. And it had been secure. Suddenly she felt very alone sitting at the table, watching the guests enjoy their meal, speaking a language that was still foreign to her.

It wasn't long before Rafaela ushered two young men to her table. "This is Carlos Ortega," she introduced the shorter of the two. He had a hook nose and thin face, but a pleasant wide smile. "He makes lovely jewelry, Rosie. And this is Alfredo Cardona," she presented the taller one. Rosie noticed that he was trying very hard to hold in a paunchy stomach. "He is a jewelry merchant and he sells

Carlos' creations. They are very good friends and will entertain you tonight," she said and flitted away.

"*Hablas español?*" asked Carlos.

"*Poquito. Muy poquito*," she replied.

"I speak a little English," Carlos forced out slowly.

"Yes. And I, also," announced Alfredo.

Rosie quickly realized that they were competing for her.

"You are the sister of Danny?" asked Carlos.

"Uh, yes. *Sí.*"

"Cordoba pleases you?" asked Alfredo.

"Very much. *Mucho, mucho. Muy bonito.*"

They both seemed pleased with her attempt at Spanish, and her appreciation of their city.

"*Mañana, vamos a* . . . uh, tomorrow, *en la noche*—at night, Alfredo and I, we are pleased to invite you to see the *bodegas* of Cordoba. That will be good?"

"Yes. It's very nice of you. *Muchas gracias.*"

Carlos and Alfredo nodded at each other, proud to have scored another point in their favor.

In spite of the language difficulties, Rosie was grateful for the cheerful company. Neither one of the young men attracted her, but she was flattered by their constant, effusive attention. As their friends arrived, they introduced her as though she were a visiting fairy princess, having descended to bless their city with her magical presence.

The restaurant crowd grew considerably younger as the night grew older, and Danny slipped on some rock music in the background.

"I never thought I'd hear Peter Frampton in Cordoba," she said to Danny, who stopped by her table in a free moment.

"The international language," he laughed. "I don't play it until the older guests have already gone home."

"I think you're trying to turn this lovely restaurant into a disco!" she teased, as a few couples got up to dance.

"The Señora doesn't mind. She's always had a lively crowd of young people here," said Danny. "And I think secretly she likes the music."

"Oh, Danny, there's something I was supposed to tell you," she suddenly remembered, but Danny had just turned around to greet a new arrival. She looked up in astonishment as she heard Danny say, "Well, I'll be. Look who's here, Rosie. Our musical friend from the Prado."

Juan de Arévalo was wearing a white collarless shirt open at the neck, and she could see the black hair of his lean, tanned chest contrasting against it. There was an undeniable animal magnetism about the man, but as attracted as she might be, Rosie resented the cool, appraising look that seemed to say he was absolutely sure she wanted him. The supreme self-confidence of his manner alone made her wary.

Carlos and Alfredo greeted him in unison and both stood up to shake his hand. It was obvious from their reception that he was something of a local hero and he acted accordingly. Without waiting for their invitation, he pulled up a chair and sat himself next to Rosie. She could see that the men resented his intrusion but were afraid to cross the boundaries of good manners and his celebrity status to tell him so.

The Spanish was flowing too fast for her to comprehend, but she picked up a few words as they spoke: *París*, *Nueva York*, *guitarra*, *música*, and gathered he was telling them about his recent concert tour. She could also see, by the way Carlos and Alfredo deferred to him, that they were not at all close friends, and that sharing a table with Juan de Arévalo even awed them a little. As they confided to her later, he had never even spoken to them before.

While he did not look directly at Rosie, he moved his knee so that it pressed up against hers. She angrily moved her leg away and blushed deeply. He turned to her with a mocking smile. "I hope nothing I've just said offended you."

"Why should it?" she shot back, wondering if indeed he had said something offensive in Spanish that she had not understood.

"The scarlet color of your lovely face, Señorita."

"Your manners are abominable," she muttered under her breath. "If your guitar playing was as bad, you'd be out of work."

He seemed pleased at having riled her and enjoyed her quick comeback. "I'm delighted to discover you have a mind behind that sinfully pretty face."

The conversation stopped abruptly as Rafaela appeared at the table. Carlos and Alfredo exchanged worried glances and studied their wine glasses nervously. A few people from the next table, Rosie noticed, were also watching them apprehensively. She had never seen Rafaela angry, and the sight of it was a shock. She spoke in Spanish, but Rosie had no trouble understanding. Each word was spoken slowly and with emphasis. "Señor Arévalo," she said, "you are not welcome here."

"Congratulations on your fine marriage, Rafaela," he replied cordially in English as though he had not heard her. Rosie suspected the English was for her benefit. "Did your husband tell you we met on the road?"

Danny, noticing the hush that had descended now on the entire dining room, joined Rafaela who was glaring at Juan. "Yes, he told me," she said and turned to Rosie. "Please, come with me for a moment, Rosie, into the kitchen. I must talk to you."

Before she could protest, Rosie found herself heading toward the kitchen with Rafaela. "Danny told me that this Arévalo seemed interested in you," she was speaking with short breaths, and her hands were clasped together tightly to keep them from shaking. "That man is a fine guitarist, but he is a very bad person—cruel, inhuman, unscrupulous with women. It does not matter who he hurts. I hope you will not be angry at me for interfering, but I feel responsible for you—like you are my own sister and I do not want you to be hurt. Danny told me what his friend did to you and this man, well, I think he is capable of worse. You mustn't get involved with him."

"Don't worry," Rosie assured her. "I think he is obnoxious and very rude besides."

Rafaela breathed easier. "Ah, then you have good sense.

Your parents have raised you and Danny very well. You both have good sense about people!"

When Rosie returned to the table, she saw that Arévalo was standing up about to leave. "Lovely Señorita Powell with the green eyes," he surveyed Rosie again in his careless, penetrating manner that made her feel giddy. "Perhaps we will meet again soon, but I am afraid it will not be at the Conejo Blanco." He reached for her hand and his touch sent a searing shock wave down to her toes. It was infuriating that such a horrible man could affect her that way when perfectly nice young men like Carlos and Alfredo did nothing for her.

Juan turned to Danny and said, "It was a genuine pleasure to see you again," and shook his hand. Utterly bewildered at how to handle the tense situation, Danny simply nodded.

Juan then held out his hand to Rafaela, but she would not take it, nor would she meet his eyes. Watching her for a moment, he took a deep breath, paused, then said softly, "Will you give my kind regards to your mother?"

"Never!" she hissed and glared angrily at him. But he looked past her to the kitchen door where Señora Gómez stood motionless watching him.

After he left, Danny put on a lively Rolling Stones album and soon the Conejo Blanco was back to normal. Determined to get to the bottom of the mystery, Rosie mustered all her high school Spanish together to pump Carlos and Alfredo about Juan de Arévalo.

"*Muy rico!*" they both laughed, rubbing their fingers together to indicate great wealth. She learned, in a fragmented way, that the Arévalos were one of the wealthiest landowning families in Andalusia, their nobility dating back to the Christian reconquest of Spain. They told her that his *palacio* in Cordoba boasted sixteen patios and a famous art collection. The art intrigued Rosie more than the patios, but she surmised that patios must be a sign of status. The Arévalos were also famous for vineyards that produced the finest wines in Andalusia. Juan's mother, now deceased, had been a third cousin of the queen of Spain, and his father, who had died last year, left him the title of *marqués*."

While all this statistical information was interesting, it did not come close to explaining the emotionally charged scene that had taken place in the restaurant. In her broken Spanish, Rosie indicated that she would like to know why Juan de Arévalo didn't get along with her sister-in-law, Rafaela.

The two young men exchanged a harried glance that asked a question, then solved it quickly as they both looked at Danny serving drinks behind the bar.

"It is a subject, not so . . . uh, easy," said Carlos.

"It is not for us to tell it to you," added Alfredo.

"Yes," agreed Carlos. "If Rafaela want you to know it, she will tell it to you."

Satisfied with their handling of the explanation, they both ordered another carafe of wine and drank it down quickly, hoping her embarrassing questions had ended.

Chapter Two

THE NEXT MORNING everyone put in bids to take Rosie sightseeing, but she finally convinced them that she'd prefer to take her sketch pad and explore on her own. Since her arrival in Madrid, she had been constantly accompanied by Danny, and now living under the same roof with his wife and her mother, she felt the strong need for a breath of freedom, some time alone to drink in all the new sights.

Being an artist had made Rosie self-reliant, and nothing was more natural than wandering about with a sketch pad, "taking notes" of her surroundings. But she soon discovered that subtle shadings of grey pencil on a white sheet did not do Cordoba justice. The essence of the city was in its colors—bright, vivid contrasts of pure pigments splashed on a white primed canvas. Grey tones did not exist here. Sitting in the Orange Tree Courtyard of the Great Mosque, she found her mind wandering away from the structure and began sketching a face. It wasn't until she was half finished with the drawing that she realized she'd made a perfect likeness of Juan de Arévalo.

Her immediate reaction was to rip out the page and crumple it up. How like that arrogant, rude man to intrude into her sketchbook, uninvited! But her own ego stopped her. It was a good sketch and she mused that in a few months, when she was back in Wichita, she would be glad to have it on its merit alone.

She studied the powerful lines of the face before her: the deep-set haughty eyes, the upper lip that curled in a mocking grin. Whatever Rafaela's complaint was against this man,

Rosie had no doubt that the anger was well deserved. She did not even need Rafaela's sisterly advice. Juan de Arévalo was a man to avoid.

She slammed her notebook shut on his insolent smile and wandered out into the street. A passing horse-drawn buggy pulled up alongside her, driven by a white-haired man in a jaunty black Cordovan hat. "You like to tour Cordoba?" he asked her.

"Why not!" she said impetuously and climbed into the back seat. He clucked to the horse and they went trotting off down the street.

What an inspiration, she congratulated herself. It was a fine afternoon, and what better way to see the city than from a horse-drawn buggy. Her driver turned out to be an enthusiastic, if not particularly well-informed, guide. He slowed the horse down often in front of homes with beautiful patios. "Even the most humble homes in Cordoba are filled with flowers," he said with pride. She was beginning to understand that a Cordovan patio represented more than status; it was the popular art form. How to design an outdoor enclosure using pots of flowers was more of a challenge than designing a painting!

Then he drove to the ancient Corredera Plaza where bullfights had been fought under the hard eyes of the Roman soldiers. It was a square surrounded on all sides by mellowed brown buildings of four stories, with a shady arcade at the ground level. Geraniums and carnations were so thickly hung from the balconies that the windows were barely visible. The sight took Rosie's breath away and she made a mental note to return with canvas and paints.

They passed by the magnificent palaces of the Marqués de Viana and the Marqués de Carpio. The driver told her that she must return on her own to visit these historic homes that were now open to the public.

Not far away, he pointed out another elegant residence that occupied the larger part of a small plaza. "The *palacio* of the Marqués de Arévalo," he informed her. "But it is not open to the public. The current marqués still lives there, the famous guitarist, Juan de Arévalo."

Rosie's heart skipped a beat. The driver was about to urge his horse on, but she stopped him. "Please, just a moment longer." She pointed to her sketchbook. "I would like to make a quick drawing."

He shrugged. "The *palacio* of the Marqués de Viana is more beautiful than this."

She quickly flipped past her sketch of Juan and started a fresh page. There was a light grey stone front, and over either side of the door were two sculptured statues of medieval warriors with swords. Above the door was an intricately designed crest.

"Not a bad likeness," said a deep voice behind her. "Let's see what else you've done." A hand snatched away her sketchbook.

It was Arévalo, and she realized with terror that he would probably see the drawing of him. She reached for her book, but he was walking away with it toward the door of his house. Leaping out of the carriage, she lunged at him. "Give that back to me, you thief."

He smiled mischievously. "You must not be so sensitive about your art. Art is for the whole world. From what I can see of your drawing of my house, you are an excellent draftsman." He held the book just out of her reach. "Or is it drafts*woman*? I'm so glad I arrived just now. I would have hated to miss your visit."

"I did not come to visit you. I didn't even know this was your house," she lied. "I thought it was an interesting structure."

The way he looked at her, she knew that he was aware of her coverup. "Strange, the drivers usually mention my name on their tours. But now that you are here, I will invite you in."

"Señor Arévalo, I have no intention of stepping inside your house!" she said angrily. "If you will just give back my sketchbook, I will continue my tour."

He ignored her comment and quickly paid the driver in sufficient *pesetas* to make him grin and tip his wide-brimmed hat.

"Come now," he returned to Rosie. "Can you really resist

the temptation to see the interior of an authentic Spanish nobleman's dwelling?"

"It would not grieve me to spend the rest of my life without ever having seen an authentic Spanish nobleman, much less, his dwelling."

Juan leaned up against one of the medieval stone warriors and let his dark eyes wander over her in his careless, disturbing manner. "Then how else will we ever be alone together?"

"I'd rather be alone in a cage with a hungry lion."

He shrugged and turned to the door.

"My sketchbook!" she hurled at him. "Give that back to me. You've no right to take it."

He opened the door and walked in, holding the sketchbook over his head. "To lure the hungry lioness," he teased.

"You *are* unscrupulous!" Rosie flushed with blazing fury at his insolence. "Just as Rafaela said."

Her words seemed to tame the confident look in his eyes for a brief second and he held out her sketchbook. "Señorita Powell, I did not mean to anger you. Please accept my apology. I am sincere in my wish for you to share a glass of wine with me. Since I saw you admiring the Goya paintings in the Prado, you might enjoy the interesting collection of his work we have here. It would be my honor to show them to you."

The unexpected humility and sincerity in his demeanor threw her off balance, and she found herself being ushered through the door and into the outer patio of the Arévalo *palacio*.

"You are a most difficult woman," he smiled at her, some of the old mischief flashing from his black eyes. "Now, let me give you a tour. This patio was originally constructed by a brother of the caliph of Cordoba." He pointed out the intricate Moorish designs on the walls. "You probably saw some of this type of work at the mosque this morning."

Rosie looked at him in surprise. "How did you know I was at the Mosque?"

"How in the world did you end up in front of my house?"

he smiled. "I paid the driver well to intercept you and bring you here."

The old fury leapt up again in her. "What a cocky, manipulative, low brute rogue you are!"

"I've been called worse things," he shrugged. "But I don't recall ever hearing all those words strung together in such a charming manner. Now, the marble for these columns was thought to have been brought here from Alexandria, Egypt," he continued as though there had been no interruption.

Every instinct told Rosie to bolt for the door, but she was fascinated by the exquisite *mudéjar* architecture and was curious to see the famous art collection. She decided to play along with him as long as the tour lasted, then she would leave. She knew that she would never forgive herself if she passed up the chance to see original Goyas in a private collection.

"You need not worry about my compromising your virtue," he assured her as they entered a large entry way. "The ancient Spanish code of chivalry prevents a man from ravishing a lady fair, unless of course, she begs him to."

Choosing to ignore his remark, she looked in wonderment around her. The ceiling was constructed of tiny squares of polished wood, each intricately painted and carved. The wide staircase that stretched to the next floor was also finely carved and inlaid with silver and marble. A huge portrait she recognized as a Goya by its powerful style hung in an ornate, gold frame.

She walked slowly up to it and examined every brush stroke. "Oh," she said with awe. "How he could put colors together!"

"If you like Goya, you must see his original sketches in the hallway. I prefer sketches to the finished paintings sometimes. They are a more intimate insight into the workings of an artist's mind."

Rosie later could only recall vague impressions of the furnishings. But the paintings she would never forget. There seemed to be a profusion of Francisco Goya paintings, sketches and etchings. Several were portraits of the illustrious Arévalo family. "My family knew him very well, of course," explained Juan.

As she often felt after visiting an exhibit, Rosie was limp with emotional exhaustion. She could never be an objective observer of art. It affected her too directly. The Arévalo art collection was the finest she had ever seen anywhere, including the Prado.

When Juan offered her a glass of wine, she gratefully accepted.

"This is where I spend most of my time when I am at home," he led her into a less formal room with dark cordovan leather furniture. For a moment she was overwhelmed by the deep burgundy red of the carpet and chairs, the bullfight paintings on the wall. But after a moment, she realized that she was in essentially comfortable surroundings.

There was a large grand piano in one corner of the room, and several ancient lutes and guitars, hand painted with floral designs, hung decoratively on the wall. Two French glass doors opened out onto a small patio with a charming fountain in the center, covered with earthenware pots of scarlet geraniums.

Juan poured her a glass of wine.

"From your vineyards?" asked Rosie.

"No. Chateauneuf du Pape. I'm afraid I am not very patriotic about the Arévalo wines. Some things others do better; wine is one of them."

Rosie settled back into the softly cushioned couch and watched Juan as he took a guitar from a case near the piano. While he tuned the instrument he seemed oblivious to her, and she was secretly glad to have an opportunity to study him. For the first time that afternoon, she was aware that he was dressed in faded levis, tennis shoes and a faded blue denim shirt. It gave him a rugged, almost American look— but he could never lose the inbred appearance of an Andalusian nobleman, the imposing grandeur of his ancestors that Francisco Goya had captured so brilliantly. The coarse denim shirt only accentuated the domineering pride of his strong, lean neck and arrogant head, crowned with thick dark hair.

She mentally sketched the long, lean muscles of his forearms and the long, tapering fingers that plucked the strings of the guitar.

With no announcement, he began to play, first strumming several flamenco chords, then plunging into a strange, haunting melody that vibrated through the room. She watched with fascination as his long, sensitive fingers caressed the strings, pulling cries of passion from the depths of the wooden instrument.

Rosie was transported—the scarlet surroundings, the haunting music—and the dark, brooding man before her, now oblivious to her presence, mystically enrapt in a world of his own creation. Yet, her artistic instinct told her that the music was meant to reach out to her in a way words never could—directly and eloquently to the heart. In it were tears and smiles, joy and pain—the tortured soul in a chaotic, swirling universe. When he struck the last chord, he looked up at her and a profound moment of understanding passed between them.

"What was the name of that?" she asked finally.

"*Romance de Amor*," he replied and placed the guitar carefully back in its case. "*Romance of Love*."

"Please, won't you play some more for me?"

"Most people pay to hear my concerts," the edge of sarcasm returned to his voice. "What are you willing to pay, Rosie Powell?"

Anger welled up in her. He had taken a beautiful, even profound moment, and cheapened it. It had all been an elaborate prelude to seduce her. How dare he use his talent to undermine her! It was—what did Rafaela call it—unscrupulous, against every code of ethics. "I think I'd better leave now," she said icily.

"Very well," he smiled philosophically. "I will show you to the door. Even give you a ride home if you wish."

Her shoulders dropped. Was he not even going to put up a fight? Fling some more sarcastic insults at her?

"I do not see you making any move to go," he raised his dark eyebrows.

She thought about the music. Perhaps she had been too hasty in her judgement. No one who was totally without a heart could possibly play a guitar like that. Could Rafaela be wrong?

He refilled her glass and sat down on the leather couch next to her.

As she looked up at the narrow, swarthy face, she realized how closely he resembled her own portrait of him. Her eyes lingered on the ruddy lips, curving sensuously into a smile, while he moved his long fingers across her throat to the back of her neck, under the long, honey-colored hair and in a swift gesture, pulled her head back and pressed his lips on hers. She tried to pull away, but he had her hair tightly wrapped around his hand and forced her down beneath him.

In a moment of panic, she realized that he could take her easily, if he so desired. She felt the powerful weight of his body on her and his free hand slowly circling her breasts and exploring the soft curves of her belly. She struggled against him to free herself.

But he misread her movements as a ploy to arouse him and he moved his mouth down her bare throat to the hollow of her neck.

"No, Juan," she murmured, trying to push him away.

His lips were moving tantalizingly down her chest as he unbuttoned her blouse.

"Please, Juan, we hardly know each other." It sounded silly, she realized the moment she said it. She was not dealing with a Kansas farm boy.

He stopped what he was doing and looked up at her.

"*Know* each other?" he repeated with a quizzical smile.

She felt the tears come to her eyes. Half of her wanted him with a hungry, passionate craving, while the other half conjured up a picture of Chip. What made him loom so hauntingly in her thoughts at that moment, she didn't know. But the pain of rejection was very real and it made her afraid. It was obvious that Juan de Arévalo's interest in her was a passing one, perhaps only a diversion to kill time while his real love, Jane Sidney, was off somewhere shooting a movie. It would be easy for him to get involved for a few days, maybe a week—but for Rosie, involvements were more complicated. She had not known enough men in her life to take them for granted. She had never even dated anyone else but Chip. Juan was moving too fast for her and she panicked.

And what Rafaela had said about him disturbed her. He had already lured her into his house by unscrupulous methods, playing on her love of art, working to undermine her with his guitar. He had probably seduced dozens of girls with the same elaborate scenario.

"I need some time to think," she managed, finding it impossible to breathe normally.

"I'll give you thirty seconds," he said reasonably.

"Juan, I can't just go plunging into things!" she said exasperated.

He sat up astride her and looked down at the small face framed in a halo of golden hair, her wide green eyes filling with tears. "I have never taken a woman who wasn't absolutely certain she wanted me, Rosa, and I'm not going to begin now." He leaned over and kissed her lightly on the lips.

"What a frightened little dove you are. It surprises me in so outspoken a young woman. He took one of her hands and kissed the tips of her fingers one by one. "Some day, my silken-skinned Rosa with the golden hair, we will write *conciertos* together on the galaxies and I shall play you as I play my guitar."

He stood up and stretched like a lion just waking from a pleasant dream and poured her another glass of wine. She sat up, rebuttoned her blouse awkwardly and smoothed down her hair.

He watched her seriously. "Now, tell me, what is there to consider about my making love to you? I can make you very happy."

"You're very sure of yourself, aren't you?" she regained some composure.

"Of some things," he said lightly. "As a bullfighter," he pointed to one of his paintings, "I was not very good. I am no match for a bull. At tennis and golf, I am average. If you ask me to draw a cat, I will make it look like a kangaroo. But at the piano," he seated himself on the piano bench and played a few stanzas of a Bach cantata. "You see, I am very good. But not good enough for concerts. On the guitar, I am nothing short of genius. I am realistic about my shortcomings and my talents, Rosa. So I do not brag when I tell you that at making love, I am also a genius."

"I'm impressed," she said sarcastically.

"I knew you would be," he ignored her sarcasm and resumed his cantata.

"What an egotist you are," she crossed over to the piano. "You really think I'll just lie down and perform for you like a trained dog?"

He kept on playing. "A trained dog is too predictable to be very interesting. You would be more like a cat, clawing ferociously and purring with pleasure."

"Rafaela told me to be wary of you. I can see why. You're really an unprincipled scoundrel!"

"Rafaela told you that?" She noticed the cocky self-assurance became slightly muted, and she wondered why the magic word "Rafaela" always brought him down a peg.

She decided to pursue it. "Will you tell me why you and my sister-in-law don't get along?"

He looked down at the keyboard and stopped playing.

"Were you two once. . . ," she could not complete the sentence for he had looked up and his angry black eyes held the words back from her.

Abruptly, he stood up and crossed the room. "There is one thing a Cordovan has more of than anyone else in the world that is worth more to him than gold. It is pride, something that you understand better than you imagine, my dear Kansas girl."

She felt weakened by his powerful stance towering over her. "I have no idea what you mean," she said defensively.

"The first moment I saw you in the Prado—it was what attracted me, not your beauty. You were looking down as your brother spoke about something I could see was causing you great pain, when suddenly you lifted your head, tossed your hair back, and looked him straight in the eye. It was a gesture of courage—of pride. A very Spanish gesture for an American girl.

"Rafaela has an overabundance of pride," he continued, "even for a Cordovan. Much more than you can ever imagine. I will respect that. If she does not wish to tell you what is between us, then I will not."

"But is there no chance that you and she will ever become friends?" asked Rosie, knowing it was futile to probe any more deeply into the cause of the dispute.

He took a deep breath and a weary expression crossed his face. "It is no longer up to me. I have tried more than once."

Rosie refused his offer of a ride home. It was not a long walk, and she needed the time to reflect on what had happened that afternoon. She was oddly attracted to the Spaniard, fascinated by his genius, but bewildered by the mystery that surrounded him and her sister-in-law. In a flash it occurred to her that Juan had left Cordoba a year ago. During that year Rafaela had met and married her brother, and Juan was reported being in love with Jane Sidney. Could it be that Rafaela and Juan had been lovers? That he had left her for the flashy actress Jane Sidney? Perhaps, like Chip, he had wanted his freedom for awhile longer and had gone off on a concert tour, leaving Rafaela alone? And during that time, she married Danny on the rebound?

Rosie felt sick inside. It was not fair to Danny. How could Rafaela do that to him? But then why was Juan de Arévalo going to the trouble of pursuing her? Was it only to make Rafaela jealous? Was he trying, in this devious way, to win Rafaela back?

If he was as unscrupulous as Rafaela indicated, then nothing would stand in the way of what he wanted, not even her marriage. Maybe *she* planned it that way.

Her heart ached for her brother Danny. Was he only being deceived into thinking he had a happy marriage when Rafaela was still in love with Juan? It angered her to think that she and Danny might both be pawns in a vicious game where Juan and Rafaela set the rules.

She reached the house before she realized with horror that she'd left her sketchbook, with the incriminating sketch of Juan, back at the Arévalo *palacio*.

Chapter Three

SHE HAD COMPLETELY forgotten that Carlos and Alfredo were planning to take her out on the town that night. They were waiting at the Conejo Blanco when she arrived.

"I'm so sorry," she apologized. "I was wandering around the town, drawing, and I forgot what time it was."

"We are in no hurry," said Carlos with a magnanimous gesture that forgave her everything. "We will be here having a sherry while you get ready."

She hurried upstairs to bathe and wash her hair and nearly ran into Señora Gómez coming down the hall.

"You had a pleasant afternoon?"

"Lovely," said Rosie. "Cordoba is a dream."

"You did some drawings?" she asked with interest.

"Yes, uh . . ."

"I would like very much to see them."

Rosie covered her mouth, and tried to think of what to say. "You know, the oddest thing, I put my sketchbook down and began to wander about, and when I came back, it was gone."

Señora Gómez looked horrified. "But that is terrible! Who would do such a thing! To take someone's drawings!"

Rosie now hated herself for having lied to Señora Gómez. Perhaps she should have confessed the truth, but it was too late and she worried about getting ready for her dates.

Danny came to her room just as she was about to leave. "So you're going out with Carlos and Alfredo tonight?"

She nodded. "The guidebooks all claim that Cordoba is famous for its *bodegas*. It should be fun."

"Well, there's safety in numbers, or, that's what Rafaela says. She insisted you go out with two at a time until you get used to Spanish men. Spanish girls are never given as much freedom as Americans. In fact, the Señora was a little leery of your dating at all. She almost never let Rafaela out of her sight when we first met.

"I did ninety nine percent of my courting under the watchful eyes of Conejo Blanco customers."

Rosie laughed. "Well, I think I can handle myself. These two should counteract each other. They're constantly competing for my attention. It's very sweet, really."

"They seem like O.K. guys," agreed Danny. "But I do worry about you, Rosie."

"Don't be silly!"

"I know that you haven't dated anyone since Chip. I'm glad you're going out tonight. It will do you good. But, you're like a babe in the woods when it comes to men."

Rosie squeezed his hand. "Would you stop worrying about me, Danny? Like Rafaela says, there's safety in numbers."

Danny forced a smile. "You're right. The little sister's all grown up now. I keep forgetting. It's just that in Kansas, Chip was so close to the family. We all trusted him to take care of you. And here, I just don't know any of these guys very well."

"But Rafaela does. I'm sure she wouldn't let me go with anyone she didn't trust. Look how fast she warned me about Juan de Arévalo."

Danny shook his head. "It's weird, I know, but that guy, for some reason, I'd trust. Don't ask me why. It's just a feeling in my bones—like you have with a good cutting horse."

Rosie wondered if he would be so quick to trust Arévalo if she told him what had happened that afternoon. But then, Juan had not taken advantage. When she protested, he had left her alone. Maybe Danny was right.

As close as they were on most things, she had never discussed sex with her brother. If he had ever known what had gone on between her and Chip, his information would have had to come from Chip. But she doubted that Chip would have had the nerve to tell Danny.

Rosie was aware of the sexual revolution that had taken over the country in the last decade, but only as a distant intellectual concept. Making love to the man she had gone steady with since she was thirteen and whom she planned to marry had seemed a natural progression and never offended her sense of morality; but a friend of hers in art school who confessed to having three different lovers shocked her. Though she had never stopped to analyze it, deep inside she knew there were boundaries of behavior one didn't cross. It was conceivable to her, at this point in life, to get physically involved with a man again, but she knew it could never be in a lighthearted, frivolous manner. She could never *make* love without being deeply *in* love.

Her dates were in bright spirits as they set off, having loosened up with several glasses of sherry while they waited for her. It was a warm night and the fragrance of flowers drifted out into the *callejas*. Letting herself flow into the spirit, she looped her arms through theirs and joined them in a round of "Hard Day's Night," giggling at their terrible pronunciation.

It wasn't until they began visiting the *bodegas* that she realized how large Señora Gómez' small restaurant was in comparison. Most of the tiny *bodegas* had only one or two tables and a bar, and practically opened, like carnival booths, onto the street.

All the noisy cars seemed to have disappeared without a trace and were replaced by the more colorful horses and buggies. Their rhythmic clip-clopping up and down the narrow cobblestone streets made the town appear to exist in another century. Like the flowers, there was a profusion of guitar music wafting down from windows, out of doors and patios. Around a corner, a group of children broke into a wild flamenco dance for the pure pleasure of stomping their feet and clicking castanets.

Rosie was glad to be out. Though neither Carlos nor Alfredo were captivating enough to make her entirely forget her afternoon with Juan de Arévalo, they clowned charmingly and paraded her brightly up the streets, introducing her to all their friends.

"This *bodega*," Carlos told her as they entered the fifth one of the evening, "is not celebrated for its wine, its sherry, or its food."

"Then why are there so many people crowded in here?" She had come to learn that each bodega in Cordoba had an individual specialty that no one else could claim. A hamburger chain, churning out identical meat patties, would have been a dismal failure in Cordoba, she concluded. Andalusians would rather starve than embrace the concept of fast food.

"You will soon see why this *bodega* is the most popular in Cordoba," laughed Alfredo.

They edged their way through the crowd. Rosie recognized familiar faces from the Conejo Blanco; some were at the different bodegas they visited earlier in the evening. Room was made for them at one of the tiny tables so that Rosie was wedged in tightly on a wooden bench between Carlos and Alfredo.

"You see that man at the bar, the one with the blue shirt and tie?" Carlos whispered to her. "He is Manuel Fuensantos."

"The flamenco guitarist?" Rosie was astonished. She never expected to see so many musical celebrities in person. First the famous Arévalo, and now Fuensantos!

"Yes, he is a Cordovan. The best guitarists and the best bullfighters are always from Cordoba. The girl next to him is Antonia Gutiérrez. She has a troupe of flamenco dancers and they have toured the world."

"Are they going to perform here tonight?" Rosie asked excitedly and looked anxiously about for a stage.

"It is possible. But if not them, there will be others. Ah! Fuensantos will have to perform now. Here is his arch rival!"

Rosie saw Juan de Arévalo walk through the door wearing a black turtlenecked sweater that made his eyes look even blacker than usual. He embraced his rival, Fuensantos, like a long lost friend.

"They don't act much like enemies," commented Rosie.

"Enemies? No. How can there be enemies in art? We used to argue who was the better bullfighter, El Cordobés or Paco Camino. They fought *mano a mano* many times in the bullrings of the world. It was not a question of who was better. One was flamboyant, a daredevil, an entertainer—but with exquisite skill. The other was a classical artist. It is now the same with Manuel Herrera and Domingo Roja. Fuensantos, you will see, is an entertainer—he plays to the crowd. Arévalo, the nobleman, only to please himself. But they both play from the heart; underneath, they are Cordovans."

Rosie watched Juan talking and joking with Fuensantos and Antonia Gutiérrez. He spoke with them in a different manner than he had to Carlos and Alfredo the night before. He respected and treated these artists as equals.

"But how can a small *bodega* like this afford to hire such distinguished artists?" asked Rosie. "They must command millions of *pesetas* for their performances."

Carlos and Alfredo stared at her in shock. "In Cordoba, one does not play for money! It is unthinkable. This is their home! These are friends!"

She saw the owner come out from behind the bar and talk to the guitarists, beaming with delight. He quickly closed the doors of the *bodega* to the rest of the public.

"They are going to play," people whispered excitedly.

"But why does he close the doors?" Rosie asked them. "Doesn't he want to attract more customers?"

Carlos shook his head in wonderment at the stupidity of her questions. "Too many people to appreciate the music is not good. Only fools pay to go to concert halls!"

After a moment of haggling over who would play first, Fuensantos took the guitar, and the noisy room grew hushed with anticipation.

Fuensantos was a small man with the shiny black hair of a gypsy, a narrow mouth and long nose. His eyes twinkled with mirth as he made a mock bow to Juan de Arévalo as though he were in a concert hall. "I welcome my famous friend back home," he winked, and everyone laughed, including Juan who enjoyed the joke at his expense. Rosie was surprised to discover that he was capable of laughing at himself.

Fuensantos played a lively, intricate piece that everyone seemed to know, and soon the room reverberated with the hand clapping and foot stomping associated with flamenco music. She was surprised to see each person tapping out some inner syncopated rhythm of his own that, when blended, made perfect unity. It was not unlike blending all the colorful flowers in one patio. Fuensantos finished with a flourish and handed the guitar with great ceremony to Juan.

The room grew hushed as Juan held his instrument and glanced at the faces across the room. Then, as though seeing her for the first time, he looked directly at Rosie. She could not take her eyes from his, so powerfully did they hold her. And when he began to play, she realized with a shock that it was *Romance de Amor*.

Not a song for hand clapping and singing along, it was a song to lose one's soul in. Rosie closed her eyes and saw the leaves of a summer maple tree just after the rain, the shining droplets of water sparkling like so many forgotten tears.

When he finished the last plaintive note, there was a brief moment while the music lingered in the air; then came the burst of wild applause.

Fuensantos had been visibly moved by the music and when Juan offered him back the guitar, he refused. "Not until I hear one more from you, Arévalo. You are a magician. Never have I heard *Romance de Amor* like that. You must be in love. Only love can make a man play such music."

Juan leaned over to Antonia Gutiérrez and whispered something in her ear that made her smile. Rosie felt a wave of jealousy. How dare he play *her* song, then flirt with another woman in the next moment? Then she realized the path her mind had followed. To be jealous of the man was as bad as admitting she might care for him. It is merely an animal attraction, she told herself—nothing more. Any woman would feel that way about him, especially after hearing his music.

He broke into a lighthearted *alegrias* while Antonia tapped out the rhythm with the heal of her shoe. In one swift movement she had whirled out onto the floor. The customers moved back to give her room. It was the "stage" Rosie had searched for in vain.

An old man watching her downed his entire glass of wine and soon, at the prodding of his friends, joined Antonia in her dance.

Rosie was enthralled. All the formal flamenco performances she'd seen had been completely choreographed with native costumes. But here was the inner spirit of flamenco— the spontaneous love of rhythm and dance. Ordinary people in street clothes, on a tiny *bodega* floor, dancing not for the money or the applause but for the pure pleasure. When Antonia sat down, a plump middle-aged woman with crooked teeth took her place, and Rosie thought she was nonetheless as graceful in her movements as the tall, exotically beautiful Antonia.

Alfredo, next to her, took up a verse of the song in a throaty raucous voice. It was impossible to understand the Arabic slur of Andalusian accent, but she realized from the laughs that followed the verses that they must have had a tinge of off-color humor, even improvisation.

Another guitar had been given to Fuensantos and now he and Juan were both playing, taking turns outdoing each other with intricate runs and chord sequences. "You see the rivalry?" Carlos commented.

"*La rubia*," someone shouted, pointing to Rosie.

"They want you to dance," said Carlos.

"But I . . ."

"Go ahead, or you will disappoint them," Alfredo urged her.

"I've taken a few flamenco lessons, but I could never . . ."

Juan was watching her, his dark eyes penetrating her like

hot coals. "For me, Rosa, dance," he commanded her.

Before she could utter another protest, she was being propelled onto the floor. After the first few tentative steps, she grew unselfconscious. The music and the hand clapping, the uninhibited pervasive mood engulfed her, did all the thinking for her, and the intricate steps came as naturally as if she had been born dancing them.

The room went crazy with enthusiasm. The idea of a beautiful blond American with emerald eyes, able to dance flamenco with an Andalusian soul, was enough to win every heart in Cordoba. They would talk about it for months to come.

She whirled around and found herself looking up into the narrow, handsome face of Juan de Arévalo, who had left his guitar to join her in the dance. The music slowed as he clicked his heels, slowly at first, then building speed, the long hard muscles of his thighs controlling the rhythm, his strong back arched like a matador, his sensuous eyes on her.

Someone threw him a wide-brimmed black Cordovan hat that he set at a rakish angle, shading his heavy-lidded, dark eyes. They circled around each other, like a pair of tigers. The *seguidilla* had become as sensual and primitive as the Gypsies who brought it from Africa. She was aware of nothing but his eyes controlling her every move and the pounding rhythm that swept her away in its throbbing beat.

When they finished, he leaned over and brushed her cheek with his lips. "Come home with me tonight, Rosa. We will continue what we have begun."

"I'll leave with my escorts," she hissed back at him with indignation. How could he be so conceited as to think she would consider leaving her dates. Besides, how could she ever explain it to Rafaela if she drove up later in a car with him.

Juan lifted his glass to her in a mocking smile, "You are a woman of principles. How admirable," then returned to the bar to resume his conversation with Antonia and Fuensantos.

When she left with Carlos and Alfredo, he did not even look up. That was all the assurance she needed to convince her that her decision had been correct. If she had gone home with him, he would have forgotten her that very night, as soon as he'd had what he wanted. And she would have shamed Rafaela and Señora Gómez by her wanton behavior.

The streets of Cordoba were quiet now. Most of the *bodegas* had long since closed down. "How about a coffee in my jewelry shop before going home?" suggested Carlos.

"Thank you, but I am totally exhausted. My poor feet are not used to all that stomping. I'd rather go straight home."

Carlos and Alfredo exchanged a glance.

"But it's right on the way," protested Alfredo. "We will have one quick coffee and you can see the beautiful jewelry Carlos makes. Then we walk you home."

There was something in the tone of their voices that she did not like, but they had been so kind to her all evening, spending so much money—it would be rude of her not to accept their invitation. Sitting in a jewelry shop certainly seemed innocent enough, and didn't Rafaela say there was safety in numbers?

Turning down a narrow *calleja* and then another, they finally reached a wrought iron gate. Carlos inserted the key in the lock and they entered quietly. "My mother is asleep in the house in back," he explained.

Rosie chided herself for being suspicious. How could a man try anything devious with his mother close by?

As she excused herself to go to the bathroom, she saw Carlos putting up some hot water for coffee. How could she have thought they were up to anything? It was all just as they said. But when she returned to the shop, Alfredo had vanished.

"He was too tired to stay, and asked me to give you his apologies," explained Carlos and pointed to the coffee bubbling on a burner. "We will have one coffee, I show you my work, and then I walk you home."

If there was someone to be left alone with, Rosie wished

it had been Alfredo instead of Carlos. There was something more sympathetic and open in his tall, slightly awkward manner.

Carlos showed her some pretty pieces of intricately worked silver and though most of the jewelry was too ornate for her taste, she could appreciate the fine craftsmanship that went into making and designing it. He was unlocking a drawer in his work table and took out a necklace that had an emerald drop on the end. "The emerald like your eyes," he said in a husky voice. "I make you a present?"

Rosie was not sure she had heard him right. "Thank you, Carlos, but no, I could not possibly accept a gift from you . . ." Maybe he wanted her to buy it?

He had walked swiftly behind her and was lifting the silky honey-colored hair up in back and attaching the clasp. "You try it on and see how beautiful." She could feel the hot breath on her neck, his clammy lips on her skin.

She spun around and faced him. "Carlos!"

"Señora Gómez does not have to know," he whispered seductively, "I will never tell her. We could have a nice time tonight," he placed a tentative hand on her breast.

She pushed it away and undid the necklace. "I would like to go home," she said firmly.

"What is wrong?" he sneered. "You do not like me because I do not play *la guitarra* and do not have a *palacio* like the Marqués de Arévalo?"

His reference to Juan angered her even more.

"I want to go home right now."

Grabbing her roughly, he held her tightly. She was amazed that such a small rodent of a man could have a vicelike grip. His arms tightened around her like tentacles as he planted wet kisses on her neck. She struggled to get loose. "My brother used to play football," she said as calmly as she could manage, "He is strong as an ox. He could kill a man, but the only time I've ever seen him angry enough to do so was because of an insult to me. A mere verbal insult," she repeated and wondered what Carlos would think if she told him that Danny had only been seven years old at the time. But it had the desired effect. Carlos stepped back.

"If you want to go home, go! *Buenas noches, Señorita.*" He led her to the gate then slammed it behind her, leaving her alone on the street, and walked back into his shop.

"I hope that woke up your mother," she yelled at him, rattling the iron gate. Then she stared down the empty *calleja*.

The wine and sherry had now completely worn off. Where was she? Had they come from the left or the right? She walked a few steps. Maybe if there was a street sign. She pulled a tourist map from her purse. Under the diffused light of a window, she unfolded it, but it only indicated main thoroughfares, not the narrow *callejas*. It was impossible to determine where she was.

Her footsteps echoed off the buildings, and the tiny narrow streets that were so friendly and colorful during the day were now eerily cold and silent, the myriad of pots with hanging geraniums casting weird shadows on the walls. At the end of one *calleja*, she found herself on but another and another, hopelessly lost in a terrifying maze.

From a recessed doorway behind her, she heard a scratching sound. She froze, then pivoted sharply only to frighten a small white dog with a black spot over one eye, who had been awakened by her footsteps. Relieved, she kneeled down and extended her hand in a gesture of friendship, and the dog trotted up to sniff her.

They quickly became friends and she hugged him to her, thinking of her own mongrel dog at home in Kansas, so far away. For the first time on her trip she was miserably homesick and the tears of loneliness welled up like a flood inside her. Men were people she'd never understand. How could Carlos seem so nice, then turn a helpless girl out into the night alone in a strange city?

Her loneliness turned into a frenzied panic as she began wandering aimlessly through the streets. The dog followed her for a short way through the streets, then returned to the security of his own doorway.

As she rounded a corner, she found herself in a small plaza. At least it is not another *calleja*, she thought optimistically and unfolded her map. With a glimmer of hope pounding in her chest, she searched for a street sign.

Just then, a small red sports car drove up to one of the houses and stopped. A tall man got out, then walked to the other side to help his female companion.

Rosie started toward them. Perhaps they could give her directions on how to get home. But as she got closer, she stopped cold. It was Juan de Arévalo and Antonia Gutiérrez.

Slipping back quickly into the protective shadows of a doorway, she tried to decide what to do. Her heart was pounding, but pride kept her from running to ask for his help.

Juan was leaning over to kiss Antonia. What if he planned to spend the entire night with her? He might disappear into her house until morning. Then another feeling crowded out the others. Jealousy. Oh, what an inappropriate time to feel that, she thought miserably. My life is at stake and I'm so caught between pride and jealousy, I can't even take an action to save myself!

Antonia stepped inside the door and waved goodbye to Juan. Rosie let out the breath she'd been holding. At least, jealousy ceased to tug on her overwrought emotions, but pride had not disappeared. Did she have the nerve to approach Juan? To have him taunt her with her *moral principles*?

While she agonized over a decision, he walked swiftly past his car to where she was standing in the shadows.

"I thought so," he pulled her out from the doorway. "Your blond hair reflects in the moonlight. Where are your two charming escorts at this late hour?"

"Oh, don't you Cordovans have some code of dignity or chivalry or something?" she said shakily.

"Are you cold?" he dropped his sarcasm and looked at her with concern.

"No."

"But you are shivering. Come," he took her hand, "I have a jacket in my car."

He helped her into the red sports car and draped his cordovan leather jacket over her shoulders. The heavy warmth of it made her feel secure.

"If I hadn't spotted you, you'd have stood there all night before approaching me, wouldn't you?"

"I didn't want to interrupt anything between you and Miss Gutiérrez," she said weakly.

"Antonia and I are good friends. We were on a concert tour together once."

"That kiss looked to me like you were more than friends," she shot back with more bitterness than she'd intended.

Juan laughed. "There is a disarming innocence about you at times, dear blushing Rosa. When I was learning to play the guitar, there were so many beautiful pieces I wanted to know and I tried everything, even those way beyond my ability. Some were more difficult than beautiful, but there were always parts that were lyrical and lovely. Years later sometimes you remember with nostalgia. You play the strains that were lovely—but to master the entire piece again, no. Does that satisfy your curiosity about me and Antonia?"

"Women and music are synonymous to you, aren't they?"

"As love and art are to you." He reached behind the seat and handed her the sketchbook. She suddenly felt very hot beneath his heavy jacket.

"Now, are you going to tell me what happened tonight with Carlos and Alfredo?"

It all came back to her, the struggle with Carlos, the frightening, aimless wandering through unfamiliar streets. As she blurted it out, she found that she could no longer hold back the tears. The harder she tried to hide her humiliation and terror, the worse it became.

He pulled her gently toward him and she laid her head on his chest, feeling the taut muscles under the sweater. He kissed her forehead and caressed her long hair and, when she finally finished the story, he lifted her chin and said, "Now, Rosa, let me see you shake out your hair, like you did that day in the Prado."

She forced a smile and obeyed him. "Ah, that is how I like you best," and he rewarded her with a light kiss on her upturned lips. It sent a searing fire through her veins. Reading the willingness of her reaction, he pressed closer, hungrily tasting the softness of her mouth, while his sensitive hands explored the silken skin under her blouse.

"There is such promise of passion in you, my Rosa. Come, I will take you to my home. Ah, how much time you wasted with those clowns tonight when we could have been in each others arms."

He turned on the ignition and, while letting the engine warm up, he pulled her to him again.

Rosie was too stunned for the moment to answer him, seething with outrage at his deceit. "Here you were pretending to rescue and comfort me like a chivalrous knight in shining armor, and it was nothing more than another ploy to get me into bed. Well, I have no more desire to spend the night with you than I did with those *two clowns*, as you called them."

She reached for the handle of the car door to get out, but he stopped her.

"I will not let you go wandering about in the night, Rosa. It is dangerous."

"How decent of you to be concerned," she said sarcastically.

"What a virgin you are," he looked at her with amusement and turned the car down the street.

"Why is it that a man assumes, just because a girl does not want to jump into bed with him, that she must be a virgin?" Rosie shot back.

"You are dying to jump into bed with me," he said nonchalantly, "but you've had little or no experience with men and you're terrified of your own passion."

"What makes you think you know so much?" she countered angrily.

"There are some things I know *very* well," he smiled at her.

"Oh, yes, I forgot—women and guitars. A genius, you

called yourself, in all humility. Well, you are wrong, I am not a virgin."

He stopped the car in front of the Conejo Blanco and looked down at her, his dark eyes sparkling with reflected moonlight. "No man has ever touched you the way I have." As if to illustrate his point, he ran his long fingers sensuously down her neck, and teased the tip of her breast. She felt herself drawn toward him as though she were as helpless as a marionette. Her lips parted in anticipation of the kiss, but he suddenly stopped and held her shoulders away from him. "Every nerve in your body is straining for me. Deny it."

"You are a conceited, mistaken man," she protested weakly.

"Conceited, but hardly mistaken, *mi amor*." She felt the searing warmth of his lips on hers and the melting turmoil of her resolve to resist him. Unable to hold back any longer, she encircled his strong neck with her arms as he devoured her mouth hungrily and the dark Cordovan night swirled mysteriously around her.

"It is late," he pulled back from her. "And your brother is waiting up for you." Juan pointed to the window above them which reflected light onto the street. "Meet me tomorrow at the Almodovar Gate at noon and I will take you on a tour of the Alcazar." He got out of the car and opened the door for her, helping her up from the low sports car seat.

"Tomorrow," she answered breathlessly and stood motionless on the curb as he climbed back into the car. What a marvel, she thought, that he could fold up those long legs into such a small car. Almost as an afterthought, she leaned down and tapped on his window. "I forgot to thank you for taking me home."

"My pleasure, Señorita," he rolled down the window and reached out to touch her lips. On a sudden impulse she kissed the tips of his long fingers, the genius fingers that could create such exquisite music.

As he drove off she realized she was still wearing his

jacket that stretched down to her knees and thought how silly she must look. Even though she was no longer cold, she pulled it around her and smiled. The sketchbook was clutched tightly to her chest. It no longer disturbed her that he had seen the incriminating portrait.

She unlocked the gate with her key and trudged through the patio and up the stairs. It was all seeming like a dream. The evening that might have ended in disaster had turned out all right in the end. And she was certain that after she explained to Rafaela how kind Juan had been to her, she would . . .

There was a clatter on the stairs as the family engulfed her. Danny was hugging her saying how worried he'd been, how late it was. Rafaela was rattling away in Spanish. It was evident she was blazing mad, but Rosie could not understand what she was saying.

"I was so worried I was ready to send out the blood-hounds," said Danny.

"I think they found me," she smiled, thinking of the little white dog with the spot over his eye.

She looked up to see Rafaela glaring furiously at her. "Oh, Rafaela, I hope I didn't worry you, Carlos and Al-fredo . . ."

"*¡No me digas!*" she stomped her foot. "It is obvious what you did. You left my friends for that devil of a man."

"Rafaela," Danny tried to calm her, "Let Rosie tell her story."

"The story is told. I saw it from the window," she turned and ran to her room, slamming the door with such force that it shook the entire house.

Chapter Four

WHEN ROSIE AWOKE the next morning, Rafaela was sitting on the edge of her bed, tears in her eyes. "Please forgive me, Rosa. We Cordovans, sometimes, we are all emotion. We do not think what we say. We do not stop to listen. I am so ashamed of myself. Danny explained everything to me last night and I wanted to apologize then, but you were already asleep. Oh, what a terrible night you must have had. And it is all my fault!"

As Rosie focused her sleepy eyes on Rafaela, the night came back to her in a flash, and she remembered her noontime date with Juan. "What time is it?" she rubbed her eyes.

"Ten o'clock. Danny and I just came back from Carlos' house. Oh, what a morning we spent there! Danny was ready to kill him, but when we arrived, Carlos and his mother are crawling on the floor, picking tiny jewels out of the carpet. It was a very funny sight," Rafaela giggled.

"What were they doing on the floor?" asked Rosie.

"We were not the first to pay Carlos a visit," Rafaela continued with glee. "Juan de Arévalo had been there early in the morning, waking up Carlos and his mother. He was so angry at Carlos for what he did to you, that he threw him across the room and upset his work table. And now the jewels are scattered all over the floor. The mother of Carlos, I have never seen her so angry, yelling at Carlos. She had no sleep last night either; you woke her up when you left! One thing you must never do in Spain is go to a man's house alone. He will only interpret it one way. I should have warned you."

Soon, Rosie and Rafaela were laughing about the inci-

49

dent like old friends—like sisters, thought Rosie happily. "I would never believe that Juan de Arévalo could be a man of honor," confided Rafaela, "but he goes up in my estimation."

"Perhaps he's changed since you saw him last," Rosie suggested.

Rafaela shook her head vehemently. "Nobody can change *that* much. I do not trust his motives, but I will concede that last night he behaved well toward you and for that I am very grateful. My mother sent Danny to his house with some special sweet cakes that she baked to thank him."

"I think Juan would like to be friends with you, Rafaela," said Rosie carefully. "I don't know what happened in the past, but maybe now . . ."

"No, Rosie," Rafaela was twisting a handkerchief nervously in her delicate hands. "There are things that go way back into the past between us. You see, Juan de Arévalo and I . . ." she bit her lower lip and then cast the subject far away. "Today, I want to make up to you for last night. After you get dressed and have breakfast, I will take you to the Almodovar Gate and we will tour the ancient castle of the Alcazar."

Remembering that she'd made a date with Juan for the identical tour at noon, Rosie tried to protest without actually telling Rafaela she was going to see Juan. She was in no mood for another sisterly lecture on his shortcomings. But it made her feel guilty to deceive her sister-in-law. Perhaps it would be best to simply say, "Rafaela, I am going to see Juan de Arévalo, and I'm willing to take the chance he will treat me fairly." But what was it that Rafaela was so unwilling to tell her? Perhaps she would do best to heed the sisterly advice. Last night had proved to her one thing— she was indeed an innocent when it came to men.

In all probability, Juan had rescued her only to press for his own advantage. It had been an act that seemed gallant only because of the circumstances. It would be naive to let a superficial debt of gratitude to him cloud her more important relationship with Danny's wife. A romance with the famous Juan de Arévalo might last a few weeks at most, but Rafaela and Danny were a permanent fixture in her life. If she were to offend Rafaela by her behavior, it would force Danny into the awkward position of having to mediate between his sister and his wife. No silly flirtation was worth that. It was hard enough on Rafaela having Danny's favorite sister move in for a visit, but having her carry on a romance with a man she despised was pushing hospitality to the limits.

She decided to forget Juan de Arévalo and make the afternoon tour with Rafaela, and the decision left her feeling oddly relieved.

But halfway through breakfast, Danny came upstairs to report that a pipe had broken under the sink behind the bar. They would have to go to a plumbing supply store to get the necessary pipe, and he needed someone to translate. Since Señora Gómez had to stay and prepare for the evening guests, it meant Rafaela would have to go with him.

That left Rosie free again for the afternoon—free to see Juan de Arévalo if she wished.

It was only ten thirty. She washed her hair and brushed it out in the warm sunshine of the restaurant patio, then went upstairs to change into some comfortable jeans and a sleeveless, pink-flowered peasant blouse. After turning the alternatives over in her mind, she decided to stick to her original decision. It would be best all around not to see Juan. More was involved than just Rafaela's feelings. She had to be honest with herself. It was impossible to be indifferent to Juan's advances for very long. It struck a chord in her that was too powerful to ignore. And she was not sure if she'd be able to handle it when he left her, as he most certainly would in time. She was not ready to face another Chip.

The afternoon could be better spent scouting out places to paint, than falling hopelessly in love with a confirmed rogue. Instead of limiting herself to the greys of a sketch pad today, she took a cloth satchel just large enough for a tray of watercolors, some brushes and a watercolor pad.

It would be little more than sketching in color, but much more satisfactory for capturing a town as colorful as Cordoba.

Just as she was getting ready to leave, Señora Gómez rushed up to her with her sketch pad. "You left this in the living room last night; I was afraid you might forget it."

"Oh, thank you," said Rosie, "But I am going to work in watercolor today. I won't be needing it."

"I hope you don't mind," said the Señora with a guilty expression, "but I wanted to see your work and so I looked."

Rosie suddenly remembered the sketch of Juan de Arévalo. Would the Señora think that she had him pose for it? The truth was she had done the drawing from memory. But she *had* spent the afternoon with him. The last thing Rosie wanted to do was lie again to Señora Gómez.

"It is a fine likeness of Juan," she said. "Please, Rosa, sit down with me for a moment."

Rosie hoped she wouldn't ask any more questions about Juan. It was so silly now, especially since she had decided not to have anything more to do with him.

"Do not worry too much about what Rafaela says about Juan," Señora Gómez began with difficulty. "He was once the cause of great pain for her, but I do not believe that he even knew it then. I have always felt that, underneath, there is an honest man, maybe even a good man."

Rosie looked at the gentle face of Señora Gómez. Strange that she would sympathize with a man who treated her daughter badly. "I do not have any intention of seeing Juan again," she said honestly. "And I don't want Rafaela to be angry with me. She is much more important to me than he could ever be."

Señora Gómez looked out the window for a moment and sighed, then turned back to Rosie. "Rafaela has a quick temper. I was like her at that age. Very proud. All my emotions I wore like a fine dress to a parade. And once I did not much like the Marqués de Arévalo and his haughty manner. My words may have influenced Rafaela. But people do change. He is a great musical genius, and to do that you must have profound depths to your soul. You are both artists . . . Perhaps for each other you will be the one great love. But most important, you must make up your own mind, Rosie. You are an intelligent girl with good sense. If *you* like him, that is all that matters."

It was a pleasant walk through the old quarter of Cordoba. Rosie could look back now and laugh at her terror from the night before. In the daylight, nothing could have been friendlier than the sparkling whitewashed houses and the cascading flowers dancing with light in the sun.

In a moment as impetuous as her decision the day before to take the carriage ride, she took out her tourist map and located the Almodovar Gate. Perhaps Juan had even forgotten about their date and wouldn't be there. But she was still curious about him. And Señora Gómez' words seemed wise. She *should* make up her own mind about the man before pronouncing judgement.

The Almodovar Gate was in the Roman Wall that separated the old Jewish quarter from the rest of the city. Rosie was delighted with the spot, and since it was a few minutes before noon, she took out her watercolors. There were three terraced reflecting pools strewn with water lilies and lined with cypress, willows and rose bushes. The statue at the very end was dressed in the toga of a Roman statesman, but he had the noble, aristocratic features of a Spaniard. The plaque announced that he was the poet-philosopher Seneca, one of the most celebrated Spaniards of all time.

The painting did not go well. The structure was easy to draw, even the statue, but the colors were more elusive and subtle than she anticipated. Through much mixing, she finally got the correct brownish tone of the wall, but when the paint dried, it flattened out much too light. She was silently cursing her inability to get the effect she wanted when she heard Juan's voice beside her.

"I'm sorry I'm late, but my agent called from London. Julio Cantaron was scheduled to do the *Concierto de Aranjuez* with the London Philharmonic in two weeks, but he is ill. They are asking me to fill in."

"Will you go?" There was a twinge of disappointment that he might be leaving so soon.

"Would you miss me?"

"Not at all," she said flippantly.

"Ah, then perhaps I should not go. You would forget all about me the moment I left you," he laughed and stared at her painting. "Now why do you paint the Roman Wall that color? It is much too yellow."

"I thought art was not in your line of genius," she said testily. It was unfair of him to zero in so quickly on her trouble.

"One cannot live a lifetime surrounded by Francisco Goyas and not come away with some knowledge," he shrugged. "I could not tell you *how* to do it, but I know that it is wrong. The structure is right, the color is wrong." Rosie squinted up at the sun, then back at the gate. "It's the light here," she announced. "In Kansas, the light is constant. It doesn't change the texture of things like it does in Cordoba. I will mix one color, sure that it's right, and a few moments later, it changes."

"Yes, blame the light because you cannot capture it," he lectured her, "or perhaps our Cordovan water does not mix with your American paint. I might as well criticize Joaquín Rodrigo because he wrote his *Concierto de Aranjuez* too complicated for me to play."

Rosie was skirting the fringes of anger. Who was he to assume that her own talent was any less than his? "And am I to assume then that you played the *Concierto de Aranjuez* through perfectly the first time you attempted it?" She rinsed out her brushes in one of the reflecting pools.

"Ah, but you must not take criticism ungratefully. It can be very helpful to an artist."

"There is a difference between being helpful and putting someone down," she squeezed the brushes to get all the water out and twisted the ends to make them hold their shape.

"You are sensitive about your work," he smiled. "That's a good sign. It means you are serious, and I could see from your sketchbook and even this misguided watercolor that you have talent—perhaps even the makings of genius. I was teasing you, yes, Rosa, but not putting you down. Did you ever consider that color in a painting does not necessarily have to imitate life. How you *feel* towards something may affect the color value you give to it."

It was, in fact, a subject which deeply concerned her, but she was surprised to hear the idea suggested by Juan. "I know *exactly* what you mean," she said excitedly. "People in Kansas used to criticize me all the time for changing true colors. Once I painted a portrait of a woman in a green dress, only I made it lavender, and her skin, which was olive, I made a translucent white. I explained to her that those colors reflected something about her inner spirit, that it was the way *I* interpreted her. But she could not understand the concept of using colors symbolically."

She noticed that Juan's eyes were sparkling with a new brilliance she had not seen before. "It is the same with music; people do not understand me either! In the time of Mozart, musicians were supposed to *interpret* music, improvise from the score that was written. That was how their performance was judged.

"When they go to a concert now, they expect every note to be played exactly as it is written. They all own long-playing records that they have memorized, note by note. If I go into a concert hall and improvise on a theme of Bach, I am criticized roundly for deviating from the master."

Rosie spoke quickly, her thoughts pouring out. "Artists have the same trouble with photographs. Everyone with a flash camera can make their own reproduction of a scene, and they expect an artist to make the same faithful copy. It leaves nothing to the imagination or emotions."

Their eyes were locked as though in an embrace, so closely aligned were their thoughts. "It is why I play flamenco music, Rosie. Flamenco is one of the few musical forms where one can, and is expected to, improvise and interpret, to create something unique. There is freedom for me in flamenco, as in no other music." He stopped speaking and stared at her with surprise. "I have never said these things before, though I've thought them many times. Why do *you* bring them out in me?"

She flushed deeply, as though he had seen her naked, for she too had bared a private, secret place in her mind to him.

Chip had never shown any interest in her art. They had never even had a conversation that came close to this one. Talk was always confined to immediate subjects: where they would go for dinner, what time they would meet, gossip about mutual friends. What really mattered—her feelings about art—she had never been able to share with him.

"Did you exhibit your paintings in Kansas?" Juan asked her with renewed interest.

"I had a few shows," she said sadly. "The photographic landscapes of farmhouses sold very well, but then I began to rebel. I painted pink farm houses with purple cows flying over the fields and cows jumping over the moon."

"Ah, that was *you* who wanted to leap over the moon," he laughed.

"Yes," she said breathlessly. How quickly he had known what she meant, without having even seen the work. "I wanted to make symbolic statements with my work. But it was terribly misunderstood and laughed at. Finally, I had to take a job in an ad agency to make some money. Commercial art is a lot of drudgery: paste-up, specing type, designing brochures. I did very little illustration, except for a furniture store downtown. Drawing sleeper sofas is not very exciting."

"But why didn't you go to New York where the new movements are happening all around?" he asked with surprise. "You are too good to let your talent disintegrate in a desolate place where nobody appreciates it!"

She pressed her lips tightly together, remembering why she had never left Kansas, why she had not left there until this trip to Spain. Chip. Chip had kept her there. Security and the promise of marriage had taken precedence. The thought of Chip and his desertion suddenly made her look up into Juan's dark eyes with a new fear.

"So you may go to London," she said suddenly. "Your actress lady friend, Jane Sidney lives there, doesn't she?"

"At times. Right now she is in Acapulco, Mexico," he pushed a lily pad absently with a dead branch.

"Filming a movie there?"

"No, she is there with her latest lover, the director of her last picture." There was a tone of unconcern, even indifference in his voice. Rosie wondered if it did not conceal some deeper emotion.

"And you didn't fly into a jealous Spanish rage at her betrayal of you?"

He smiled indulgently. "Jealous rages are not in my repertoire." He was watching how carefully she wiped her watercolor tray clean.

"Then what was it you flew into this morning at Carlos' jewelry shop?" Her eyes were twinkling with mirth.

"Justified anger. I would have done it for anyone. Carlos acted stupidly and placed you in great danger." Juan walked over to the statue of Seneca and made a mock bow. "Stoically speaking, sir, would you have done less for this damsel in distress?"

Rosie laughed at the sight of him so seriously addressing the statue. Placing her watercolor materials back in the cloth satchel, she ripped the painting from the pad and threw it in a trash can. Juan was surprised at her action. "I am not as sensitive about my work as you imagined, you see."

"What you have just done takes a lot of nerve," he said with admiration.

"No more than you would do in a recording session if you did not like the first cut of a piece of music," she replied.

He put a casual arm around her. "If you stay here long enough, you will get it right. Even El Greco was not a native of Spain, but he learned to paint us."

"And Bizet, who wrote Carmen, was a Frenchman," she added playfully.

She liked the masterful way he guided her through the streets. She had never felt so protected by a man and wondered if he was really arrogant, or merely self-assured. Of course, this was his home town; he had the confidence of knowing exactly where he was going. But she suspected he would be the same in London or Paris. Not even the mausoleumlike skyscrapers of Manhattan would intimidate the Marqués de Arévalo.

The Alcazar, like the Great Mosque and the Roman Wall, was constructed out of the same soft, golden brown stones that had eluded her usually perceptive sense of color. She was surprised that for a palace it was not larger, more grandiose. In size it could have been a mansion in Wichita, but for the luxurious gardens that stretched away from it and down to the Guadalquivir River. She and Juan walked silently down the shaded paths, by the trickling fountains and reflecting pools. It occurred to her that everything in Cordoba was elusive: the changing blue shadows on the narrow, flower-lined paths; the delicate mutable colors of the roses swaying with a gentle breeze in the sunlight. Nothing was quite as it seemed, including the intriguing, dark handsome man who walked beside her.

They climbed a perilous narrow stairway that wound up a tower until she was quite breathless. But the view of the city was well worth the effort. Over the red tiled rooftops, they could look over an enormous expanse of beige rolling hills covered with cultivated lines of grey green of olive trees.

Juan pointed just beyond the Almodovar Gate and said, "Out there are the ruins of the great Medinat az Zahra, where the Moorish caliph built a palace for the woman he loved. They say the sultan had a hundred rooms just to himself, and the roof was supported by over 4,000 columns."

"I would love to see it," said Rosie enthusiastically.

"You would be disappointed. It is little more than ruins, now. The Moors, unlike the Romans, did not build for eternity."

"Is it far away from here?" Rosie was undaunted by his

skepticism. The idea of sultans and harems had taken hold of her imagination.

"About five miles out of town. Once, when the caliph was expecting a foreign dignitary, he had the entire road lined with musicians, dancing girls and servants holding umbrellas to shield him from the sun," Juan was amused at her winsome reaction to his story.

"It's all so exotic," she said, seating herself precariously on the edge of the wall and looking out across the city.

"In everything I've ever read about Spain, I never expected it to affect me this way. The photographs never do it justice. They don't capture how it makes you *feel*."

He sat down next to her on the ledge. "Perhaps you are feeling something more than just an appreciation of the scenery?" He ran his hand down her bare arm, and the effect on her was like an electric shock. She stared up at his darkly handsome, chiseled features framed by a cobalt blue sky, the warm afternoon wind tousling his thick black hair. He cupped her face in his strong hands and leaned down to kiss her. It was dizzying. She grasped onto the narrow ledge to keep from careening off the tower, but he took her hand and placed it around his neck. "I would not let you fall, my lovely Rosa. Not now, when you are beginning to realize that you are in love with me."

She withdrew her hand. "In love! Hardly. Or can you accept the vague possibility that a woman might not be susceptible to your tremendous charms?"

"Why do you fight it?" he asked, amused.

"You may fascinate me, yes. But I'm not anywhere near to being in love with you!"

He stood up and looked down at her. She did not like this angle, having to gaze up at him that way. It made her feel very small and powerless. She jumped to her feet and faced him more squarely with her clear green eyes.

"The Andalusian pride in the girl from Kansas," he laughed and took her hand to help her down the narrow stairway. "You're not afraid of me, are you, Rosa?" he asked suddenly.

"Afraid of you!" she threw back her long blond hair. "Not in the least."

"I'm glad to hear that," he smiled. "Then you would not be adverse to taking a ride this afternoon out to my vineyards. I have some business to take care of with the foreman. And if you wish, we can stop at Medinat az Zahra. It's on the way.

The ruins of the sultan's palace, as Juan had predicted, left little to recall the sumptuous residence it must have once been. And it gave Rosie a chill to think that 25,000 people had once lived and worked there, and they were all gone now, without a trace.

She was enjoying the drive out of the city in Juan's flashy red sports car. They had the top down and, though he drove very fast, whizzing past cars on the winding road, she was not afraid. He controlled the small car like he controlled intricate stanzas of music.

The old villa was set back in the hills behind a whitewashed wall covered with red bougainvillea. Not as richly elegant as his ancestral home in Cordoba, the villa, nevertheless, had a rugged charm, and the setting under shaded oaks reminded her of the Powell family home in Wichita. She wished Danny were here to see it with her and felt a pang of guilt that Rafaela might be angry with her for coming. What had she said only that morning—never go into a man's house alone? What was there about Juan that made her discard every precaution?

"Do you also have horses here?" She thought again how Danny would love this place.

"Yes. There is a fine stable in back. Do you like to ride?"

She nodded. "But I was mainly thinking about my brother. He is crazy about horses; he used to ride the rodeo circuit back home."

Juan seemed pleased. "Good. Then I will see that he has an open invitation to come here and ride my horses. They need the exercise and I am home so rarely."

"That's very generous of you," she said with surprise. "You just met him!"

"It does not take me long to make up my mind about people." The pathway up to the house was lined with blooming white oleander bushes, and the garden sparkled with roses and orange trees.

"Do you know that this morning Rafaela told me she thought you might have changed," she said lightly, watching for his reaction.

He raised his dark eyebrows, but didn't look at her.

"And Señora Gómez spoke to me. You know, in a strange way, I think she even approves of me seeing you."

He turned to Rosie with a look more serious than she anticipated. "Then perhaps there is a chance for me."

"What do you mean by that?" It occurred to her that if he were still in love with Rafaela and wanted to steal her from Danny, he might be using Rosie as a go-between. And if he were as cruel and unscrupulous as Rafaela suggested, he would not stop at using Danny as a lure, offering his horses as bait.

"You glare at me like I am the Devil. I assure you I am not," he laughed. "Now let me show you the villa."

Above the blue tiled mantelpiece in the living room was a portrait of a man who looked very much like Juan though he was dressed conservatively in a business suit in the style of the 1940s. "Your father?" she asked. He nodded. "I can see the strong resemblance."

"We are very different men," he said in a way that halted any further discussion.

"Are there any portraits of your mother?"

"No," he said with an even greater abruptness and turned away to show her the outer patios.

Rosie tried to imagine why he was so sensitive about his parents. From what he said about his father, she gathered they hadn't gotten along. Had his father objected to his music, his lifestyle . . . or even, perhaps, Rafaela? Rosie did not know much about class differences, but certainly in Spain the lines were more clearly drawn than in America.

After he concluded his business with the foreman and they had enjoyed a delightful meal of cold meats and fresh fruit served by one of the maids, it was nearing twilight and the hills were awash with soft gold light. Juan suggested they return to Cordoba before her family began to worry, but Rosie felt a sad reluctance to leave the pleasant villa and told Juan so.

"I knew you would like it here," he hugged her. "I'm glad you came with me. We will come back here again." He turned the car down the dirt path, but as they rounded the first bend, there was a loud bang from the engine. Juan got out and opened the hood. Rosie could see smoke swirling out from where she sat.

"I had my mechanic work on that all yesterday," he said angrily. "I'll have to send my foreman into the village and hope the mechanic hasn't gone home yet. Even then, I don't know if he will have the necessary parts."

The foreman returned an hour later looking exasperated. He had been to the closest village, but found the garage already closed. The garage in the next town was open, but the mechanic was too busy to come. The only option left to them was to take the truck for the two and a half hour drive back to Cordoba. But it was also in need of repair, and Juan feared that if they started out they would run the risk of being stalled on the road at night.

"What about an auto club, or perhaps a rent-a-car service?" suggested Rosie.

"You are in Spain, not Kansas, *mi hermosa*," he laughed.

"How about my calling my brother. Perhaps he could drive out here to pick us up."

It was now 6:00 PM and when she reached Danny, the restaurant was just beginning to receive dinner guests. It was impossible for him to get away. "Why don't you just spend the night there," he suggested, "and I'll drive out in the morning."

"But, Danny, what would Rafaela and the Señora *think*?" Juan was in the next room and she hoped he hadn't heard.

"I'll explain it to them. Don't worry. I'd rather have you out there than travelling these country roads at night in a truck that might break down. Your safety means more to me than your virtue. Now, put Juan on the phone."

She hoped he wouldn't give Juan some brotherly advice

or threat about taking advantage of his innocent sister. The situation was embarrassing enough as it was. But from what she could glean from Juan's side of the conversation, it was purely mechanical talk. Danny was finding out where to pick up the part he needed. Rosie smiled, thinking how her brother would be delighted to get his hands inside the engine of Juan's red sports car. And she was also thrilled at the prospect of his coming out to see the Arévalo vineyards and taking advantage of Juan's offer to let him ride his horses. Whatever her own mixed feelings about Juan de Arévalo were, she somehow liked the idea of his becoming friends with her brother.

The cook prepared them a beautiful meal of native Cordovan dishes, lamb *a la caldereta*, wild asparagus *en cazuela* and the Spanish soup specialty, *gaspacho*. The wine from the Arévalo vineyards was delicious, much better, she thought, than the Chateauneuf du Pape, and Rosie told him so.

"Have you been to see the Pope's palace, the Chateauneuf du Pape in Avignon?" he asked her.

"This is my first trip to Europe. I'm still getting used to Spain!"

"Ah, but you must plan to go to France. Every artist must go to France, especially Avignon with the nearby Pont du Gard. There is a wonderful inn right on the river, where the food is delicious—a very romantic setting."

She looked across the table at him, the candlelight flickering in his dark eyes. It was hard to imagine anything could be as romantic as sitting across the table from Juan de Arévalo, no matter where it was. She wondered about the girl he had shared that restaurant with: Jane Sidney or Antonia Gutiérrez or perhaps some sparkling-eyed Parisian actress. Had any woman ever held his attention for long? Had Rafaela tried and failed?

A cheerful fire had been lit in the living room. Juan poured them two small glasses of cognac and then picked up his guitar. If he planned to seduce her that night, he was certainly not in any hurry. Listening to the music, she stared at the flames reaching up like so many scarlet flowers, a reflection of the flamenco chords from his guitar. How many other women had sat here with him, captivated by him and his passionate *seguidillas*, wondering how life would be with such a man. There would be many nights like this, quietly sitting by a fire, concerts in the exciting capitals of Europe, side trips to romantic places, riding horses through his vineyards.

She stopped herself. It was too easy to paint herself at his side in that pleasant picture, and Arévalo was not the kind of man to tie himself down to one woman. He might be amused by her for awhile, but eventually a more exciting woman would command his attention. If Rosie could barely admit that she was pretty, she did not have the confidence to consider herself an alluring beauty like Jane Sidney, and she was sure that was what appealed to him in the long run.

"Would you like to take a walk in the garden?" he broke into her reverie. "The nights here are softer than anywhere in the world."

She was thinking that "soft" was a strange word to describe a night until she stepped outside. The gentle fragrance of jasmine and orange blossoms wafted over them like an intoxicating perfume. The black sky was like a velvet mantilla jeweled with stars.

Juan slipped his arm around her waist and drew her close, kissing her tenderly at first, then with increasing passion, his strong, knowing hands caressing the soft flesh under her blouse. Like the day at his house in Cordoba, she felt manipulated like the strings of his guitar. Only he was capable of releasing the wild primitive music held captive deep within her.

"If I go to London, I would like to have you with me, Rosa," he said huskily as they walked back to the house. "Then we could drive through France, see the Chateau country, Avignon, the Riviera and return to Cordoba through the Costa Brava. I know you would like it."

She remained silent. It was too close to her own fantasy and it made her deathly afraid.

Feeling her reluctance, he said, "Or are you not the type of woman who travels with a man who isn't her husband?"

"I . . . I don't know. I've never done it before."

"Then you do not say no?"

"No. I mean, I'm not sure. It's just a feeling in the pit of my stomach."

"You are afraid of what Rafaela and her mother will say. Afraid your brother will be angry?"

"I don't want to be the cause of any dissension between Danny and Rafaela . . . ," she said haltingly.

"But that is not the real reason," he twisted a strand of her long, soft blond hair between his fingers.

"No, it isn't," she admitted.

"It's something more complex, that goes deeper . . ."

"Yes."

"The man in Kansas?"

"Danny told you?" she straightened her back and pulled away from him. "He had no right to tell you!" She was feeling more humiliation than anger.

"You do not want me to know that a man left you once, Rosa? Broke your heart?" He pulled her back towards him.

"What did Danny tell you?"

"Not very much, actually," he caressed the nape of her neck tenderly as he spoke. "He only said that he was glad you had come to visit because there had been some sadness back in Kansas that he hoped this trip would make you forget."

"Then he said nothing about Chip! How did you know?"

"I guessed. It explains your reluctance to fall in love with me."

Humiliation now turned to outrage. "I suppose women fall so easily at your feet that you can't imagine anything but a tragic former love affair would keep them from you!"

He pulled her tighter to him, ignoring her struggles to get loose from his grip. "Do not change the subject, *mi querida*. I am going to finish what I have to say. I know very well how you tremble in my arms; I know what we could be to each other. But you hold back because you are mortally afraid that I will leave you like that other man."

"Well, wouldn't you?" she said angrily.

"Perhaps."

He let go of her and she flew into the house and up the
stairs to the room the maid had shown her earlier and
slammed the door. Throwing herself across the bed, she
buried her head in the pillows, trying to hide the tears. Why
did he have to be so brutally honest? Was there nothing
more to life than falling in love and being rejected in the
end? Where were the happy endings? Even the magnificence
of a Medina Azahara, a monument to love, ended in rubble
and ruin.

She heard Juan's footsteps on the stairs, pause at her
door, then continue down the hall. A door closed.

For a breathless moment, she wanted to call him, offer
to take him on his own terms, travel with him, be his
mistress for as long as he wanted her, no matter what the
consequences. Perhaps it was better to love passionately for
the moment and not worry how long it would last. But she
remained silent, staring up at the ceiling.

It was a warm night and the fragrance of jasmine and
orange blossoms floated up to her from an open window.
Having arrived without a nightgown, she stripped off all
her clothes and lay naked between the cool sheets, tossing,
turning, unable to find a comfortable position, too tense to
sleep.

There was a soft rap at the door. "Rosa," she heard
Juan's voice. The door opened. She froze. Did he intend
to force her into loving him for the night? She would certainly be no match for him if he wished to take her that
way. Though she could scream and wake the servants, they
would probably not come to her aid.

He was wearing a short black bathrobe tied loosely about
the waist. She suspected there was nothing underneath for
as he approached the bed, she saw his strong long legs and
broad chest covered with feathery black hair. Seating himself at the edge of her bed, he took her hand in his. "You're
not able to sleep either, I see." A hot shiver pulsed through
her veins at his touch. She wanted badly to pull him down
onto her, to cover his face with tender kisses.

"I've been thinking," she said softly.

"That's dangerous, *mi amor*, you would do better to let your feelings tell you what to do."

He felt the soft curves of her body under the sheet and began gently to pull it off.

"No," she said sharply.

He pulled his hand away and held it in midair, a mocking gesture to her modesty.

"Please, just let me say what I've been thinking, Juan. It's not that I don't want you. I do. I think I may even be in love with you. But it's all happened too fast. With Chip it took years, most of my life, to fall in love. We grew up together. He was Danny's best friend. Our fathers had even gone to high school together. There was something solid to base a relationship on. With you and me . . ."

"We are both artists. You will know some day that we have more in common because of that, than all your friends in Kansas."

"But that's not what is drawing us together," she protested.

He let his hand drop onto her belly and made a circular, caressing motion. She squirmed. "Yes," he smiled, "what is drawing us together?"

She grabbed his hand and held it still. It was clouding her thoughts. "With you and me it's the jasmine blossoms and the Medina Azahara and the cognac and. . . ."

"*Romance de Amor*," he touched her lips. "The romance of love. That is all a part of love. How dull it would be without romance." He pulled the sheet away exposing the soft curve of her breast and leaned over to kiss it. But she twisted away.

"Juan, you're confusing me!"

"*Bueno*," he smiled.

"This is all a funny game to you!" she felt the tears invade her throat. "You only want a plaything for the night. You'd tell me anything to further your amusing little seduction. You don't care how I feel, how I will feel tomorrow or the next day. Well, I won't be another toy for the marqués," she blurted angrily, "I won't cheapen my own love for a man by giving it away to some *conquistador* who would take it lightly and then cast it aside. If we ever do make love, it will be because I know you will return my love with as much commitment as passion."

He stood up. "I do not make promises I cannot keep, Rosa. I cannot promise to love you tomorrow or even later tonight. But at this moment I am desperately in love with you and want you more than I've ever wanted any woman." He stared at her for a long moment, then shedding his bathrobe on the floor, he climbed into bed with her.

She was shocked at his audacity! Had her words meant nothing to this rogue?

"Don't worry, *mi querida*," he said softly, "I am not going to take advantage. It is just too fine a night not to share it with you. I want the warmth of your soft skin touching me while we sleep. It is very beautiful to share sleep and dreams with someone you care for."

He pulled her gently toward him and she did not resist. There was no reason to because she trusted him. "Here, there is a hollow under my shoulder where you can put your head. Ah, you see? How well we fit together." He smoothed out her long hair and cradled her in his strong arms. *"Buenas noches, mi amor,"* he whispered and kissed her forehead.

Rosie lay there, afraid to move, and yet not uncomfortable. After a few moments, he began to breathe evenly and she felt all his muscles relax into a heavy sleep. He was right. It was lovely to share a night together, even without having made love. She liked the feel of his lean body, and she longed to caress and explore the intriguing contours of it. But she would not risk waking him for something she was not ready to complete. And yet, there was a completeness about them as they were, without the physical act of love—something even closer than sex could ever be. Laying beside him she imagined a painting of the two of them asleep under a tree in a green meadow somewhere, a painting Monet would have infused with soft gold light. Instead of being awake all night, she soon fell blissfully into a deep, satisfying sleep.

Chapter Five

THE MAID KNOCKED at her door. *"Señorita, ha llegado su hermano."* Rosie had no idea what time it was, but the sun was streaming brightly into the room along with the cheerful chirping of birds in the orange trees below. Juan was not there, nor was the bathrobe he'd dropped on the floor the night before. But the scent of him was still on the pillow beside her and it brought back a rush of warm feelings. Thinking about what had happened that night, she still could not believe it. How could a man have so much self-control that he would not try to make love to a naked woman sleeping by his side? But then, how would a man have as much self-discipline to learn the guitar so well? He was certainly no ordinary man.

"Señorita Powell?" the maid asked again.

"Si?"

"Está su hermano."

Her brother Danny! It finally sank in what the maid was trying to tell her! Danny was there. The maid left a tray of steaming hot coffee and sweet rolls in her room. She took a few bites and glanced around her. There was something cold, not altogether pleasant about the room in daylight. Rosie looked at the standard religious paintings then noticed a portrait over the dresser. It was a contemporary woman of at least a few decades ago, but she might have been one of the austere eighteenth century Spanish *duquesas* that peopled the portraits of the Spanish art museums. Dressed in somber black, a stout, double-chinned aristocrat with her dark hair pulled severely back, there was no warmth or kindness in the tiny black eyes. It was impossible to discern

69

her age; she could have been anywhere between twenty and forty. A single strand of cold white pearls with a gold crucifix on the end was the only adornment the woman permitted herself. Rosie studied her for a moment and decided it was this overbearing woman who gave the room such an inhospitable feeling. Whoever she was, Rosie did not like her.

When the maid returned for the coffee tray, Rosie asked about the portrait. *"Es la madre del Señor,"* the maid informed her.

"La madre de Señor Arévalo?"

"Sí."

"Este Señor Arévalo?" Rosie pointed downstairs to be sure they were speaking of the same man.

The maid nodded.

Rosie looked at the portrait again. How could it be that this was a portrait of Juan's mother? She was certain he'd told her there was no portrait of his mother in the house. How odd that he had not remembered it. But then, he had been away. Perhaps it had slipped his mind—or subconsciously he did not want her to meet this unpleasant ghost. The stern woman glared down at Rosie from her heavy gold frame. "It's lucky your son took after his father instead of you." She sniffed and turned her back on the old biddy.

Danny and Juan were down the road leaning over the red sports car, jabbering happily like two chefs over a pot of stew. Seeing Danny with grease on his hands at the engine of a car was like old times. From the time he was old enough to reach inside a car, he was always taking something apart and putting it back together.

Juan greeted her with a friendly *"Hola!"* as though nothing unusual had transpired the night before. "Your brother is a mechanical genius," he said.

"Ain't nothin' for a Kansas boy," drawled Danny in an exaggerated accent that made them both laugh. The sports car was soon in working order, but Juan insisted they go back to the villa for a hearty breakfast before driving back to Cordoba.

"I understand you like horses," Juan said to Danny as

they downed a plate of delicious eggs basted with tomatoes and olives.

"I've done a little riding," he said modestly.

"He won the cutting horse championship two years in a row at the Kansas State Fair," corrected Rosie.

It didn't take long to convince him to take a short ride around the vineyards, and since Rosie was already in jeans, she decided to join them.

Both she and Danny were awed by the beautiful Andalusian horses with their arched necks and long, wavy manes and the plush Cordovan leather saddles. "This is like sitting in a rocking chair," joked Danny.

If Rosie had expected any tension because of what had happened the night before, it simply did not happen. By the end of the morning, caked with dust and smiles, the three of them were talking like old friends.

Danny was full of a hundred questions about the horses. Where were they bred? What kind of feed did Juan use? What were the special shoes? Why were the saddles shaped as they were? Rosie had the oddest sensation as they turned the horses back to the groom—something of déjà vu: the three of them laughing, the horses, the fresh smell of hay, the easy camaraderie between Danny and Juan. Danny and Juan. That was it. Like Danny and Chip.

How often had the three of them taken off riding horses in Kansas. She thought back to what she had said to Juan the night before. About knowing a man like family. Was he using this as simply another way to get to her or to get to Rafaela?

At the last minute, Juan decided to stay at the ranch to take care of some more business and Rosie drove back to Cordoba with Danny. In a way she was relieved not to have to fill in conversation with Juan alone on the long ride back.

"One heck of a nice guy," Danny made his pronouncement. "You could do worse than to get hitched up to him, Rosie."

"Don't rush me," she protested. "I've only known him a few days."

"I only knew Rafaela a week before I proposed," he

countered, "Seemed like I'd been looking around all my life and wow!—there she was like lightning."

"Well, that was Rafaela," said Rosie, "I don't think our Juan de Arévalo is the marrying kind."

Danny shrugged. "At least he's one heck of a nice guy, and he can sure handle a horse. Boy, what would they say back home if I showed up at a rodeo with one of those Andalusian stallions!"

Curiosity dispelled any disapproval Señora Gómez and Rafaela might have had about her spending the night out at the ranch. They wanted to know every detail of the house, down to the exact kind of flowers in the garden. She told them about the distinguished portrait of Juan's father over the mantelpiece and the strange mystery about his not mentioning his mother's portrait in her room.

Rafaela and Señora Gómez exchanged a glance but said nothing.

"What an old crow of a woman she was," remarked Rosie, "when her husband was so very handsome—like Juan."

Señora Gómez' mouth fell open slightly.

"Oh, dear," apologized Rosie, "I hope the marquesa wasn't a good friend of yours!"

Señora Gómez smiled broadly at that, as Rafaela exclaimed, "¡Madre mía! The grand Marquesa de Arévalo, a friend of mine? Why, she would not consider to look down to gaze at someone not of her class."

"The artist who painted her must have disliked her, too, for her portrait is none too flattering," agreed Rosie. "We have a saying in Kansas about those people. They carry their noses so high in the air that if it rained, they would drown."

Señora Gómez and Rafaela laughed heartily.

"The marquesa, to perfection," they agreed.

Rosie wondered if maybe they did not like Juan because his mother had snubbed them.

In the next few days, Rosie had finished the Cordoba sightseeing circuit, taking in everything she could. The bullfighting museum and the paintings of the famous Cordovan bullfighter, Manolete, fascinated her the most. She stood for a long time in front of his portrait, staring at the large sad eyes, the long face. The crumbling façade of the tiny hovel where he was born was preserved as a monument to the humble beginnings of the famous Cordovan. There was something compelling in his dark eyes, an understanding of the ultimate tragedy of the human condition. It made her hope very much to be able to see a bullfight and meet a bullfighter before leaving Spain, even though she was afraid she might be upset at the spectacle.

Juan did not stop by or call in the next few days and Rosie, though disappointed, could not blame him for not wishing to continue with her. She realized that there must be hundreds of other pretty women to hang adoringly on his arm, willing to cater to his immediate needs.

Nobody could stop talking about the famous *feria* in Sevilla that was to begin the next week. "Oh, Rosie, you will never see anything like it in the world—the colors, the pageantry. It is like the world turned topsy-turvy with madness and music!" enthused Rafaela.

Two days before they were to go to the *feria*, Juan Arévalo arrived at the restaurant. "I have just returned from Sevilla," he announced with grandeur.

"And the rest of the world is getting ready to go there," said Rafaela, unimpressed.

His eyes twinkled. "I have already made arrangements, so that you cannot turn me down," he said, "I think you say in America, an offer you cannot refuse," he smiled at Rosie. Rosie was thinking that he looked awfully pleased with himself about something. Seeing him again, even after a separation of a few days, gave her an alarming wobbly feeling in the knees.

He explained that he was having two of his best horses brought down from the ranch along with several traditional Spanish costumes of the *feria*. He wanted Danny to ride one of the horses, and he would ride the other. Rafaela and Rosie would sit behind them, Andalusian style.

In addition, Juan's friend Manuel Herrera, the famous

bullfighter, would be performing at a *corrida* and he had reserved a special box for them with the Herrera family. They were all to spend the night at the Herrera mansion, and he had even made arrangements for Señora Gómez to attend the *feria* with Señora Herrera while they paraded up and down the street on horseback.

Rafaela started to protest, but then, noting the excited expressions on Danny's and Rosie's faces, gave in and ran into the kitchen to tell her mother. At the door she stopped and called over her shoulder, "You are right, Juan! We cannot refuse!"

But as she emerged from the kitchen and approached them again, Rafaela wore a more sombre face. "My mother is very happy to go, Juan, and I am accepting only because of Danny and Rosie. It is their first *feria* and with you, they will know it in a way that is unique. But for me," she looked at him darkly, "it changes nothing."

"Change is always possible," said Juan stiffly. Rosie noticed that all his usual composure was under severe strain.

"Not always," answered Rafaela coldly.

Chapter Six

THEY ARRIVED EARLY in the morning of the second day of the *feria*. Because the *feria* of Seville had the reputation of being the most beautiful in Spain, the city was crowded with visitors from all over the world.

But the excitement of the day did little to dispel the frost that Rafaela kept between her and Juan de Arévalo. Each time he tried to include her in a conversation or address a question to her, she answered coldly in one or two words. Once Rosie caught Señora Gómez pinch her daughter for a particularly curt remark to Juan. It was clear that the Señora was anxious to mend bridges while Rafaela preferred to keep them broken. It made Rosie uneasy. She wished there was something she could do or say, but the tension was too far below the surface for her to touch. Without knowing *why* they were at odds, she could only smile and pretend she did not notice it.

At the Herrera house, Rosie and Rafaela were taken upstairs to change into their costumes. Rosie chose a bright turquoise one with white flowers, trimmed in white lace. She swore she had never seen so many tiers and flounces in one dress. Rafaela picked a striking dress with a black and white polka dot bodice that billowed out into tiers of white lace, accentuated with red ribbons. Señora Gómez and Señora Herrera delighted in dressing the girls' hair in the traditional Andalusian style, pulled low over the ears and gathered at the nape of the neck with flowers.

Danny and Juan were waiting for them downstairs in tight fitting jackets, white lace shirts and cordovan leather chaps. Rosie decided that Danny, in spite of the Spanish costume, still looked like a Kansas cowboy. But Juan, in the wide brimmed black Cordovan hat set at a rakish angle and his tall, lean body and long legs, looked every bit the Andalusian nobleman that he was.

The bullfighter, Manuel Herrera, appeared briefly to say hello, but excused himself from joining them. He was to fight that afternoon and did not want to tire himself out at the *feria*. He had sent for a four-horse carriage to take them to the fairgrounds where Juan's horses would be waiting for them. The eighteenth century carriage was pale blue with gold velvet interior. Rosie felt like Cinderella, in a fairytale romance, afraid if she pinched herself, she might wake up.

All along the tree-lined parkway, tiny houses, or *casetas* had been constructed with colorfully striped canvas coverings open in front. Amateur entertainers and professional flamenco troupes wandered up and down the streets, while the brightly decorated carriages and people on horseback paraded up and down, stopping at the *casetas* to gossip with friends and sip a glass of sherry.

Señora Gómez and Señora Herrera were already chatting like old friends. They toured the park in the carriage, then settled down in the private *caseta* to watch the exciting pageantry with other Herrera relatives while Juan and Rosie, Danny and Rafaela mounted the horses.

In back of each saddle was a pillion on which the girls sat, perched sideways on the horse's rear, one arm around the man, the other on a handle projecting out from the pillion.

"This is the craziest way to sit a horse," giggled Rosie as she adjusted herself in the saddle, "But with all these skirts, I don't imagine there is another sane way to do it."

As she slipped her hand around Juan's chest, he turned back and kissed her. All the color and excitement that surrounded them slipped away in that kiss, and she was aware only of his hard body and the horse underneath them pawing to get started. "You are the most beautiful girl at the *feria*," he whispered. "Now do not dishonor me and fall off the horse," he commanded and spurred the horse forward.

"I've never fallen off a horse in my life!" she exclaimed as they trotted forward, but she wasn't too sure if this wouldn't be her first time. She felt none to secure on that precarious perch, the horse's powerful legs prancing below her.

She looked over and saw that Rafaela also seemed a bit unsteady, but Danny was in firm control and enjoying every minute.

Then suddenly Rosie saw a woman's face staring boldly at them from the crowd. She prayed Juan had not also seen it. Rosie was certain it was the actress, Jane Sidney. What was she doing in Seville? Hadn't Juan said that she was in Acapulco with her director? Had that love affair ended? Was she free again and coming back to claim the handsome Marqués de Arévalo? Until that moment, Rosie did not realize the full depth of her feelings toward Juan. If he were to leave her for Jane Sidney, she could not treat the desertion lightly.

"Relax, *mi amor*," Juan said over his shoulder. "I can feel you tense and it is no way to ride. Are you so uncomfortable?"

"No, it's wonderful, Juan," she tightened her arm around his waist and he ran his free hand across her wrists, sending shivers of pleasure pulsing through her.

"This is the best *feria* I have ever attended and I have never missed one in my entire life. I'm certain it is because you are with me, Rosa."

"Do you always have a woman riding with you?"

He gave her a wicked smile. "How curious you are about my past."

"Was there a woman with you last year?"

"Yes. And I was miserable. The woman could not ride and she was terrified of horses. I shall never make that mistake again. I kept turning around to see if she had fallen off."

"Was that Jane Sidney?" Rosie regretted her question as soon as she heard it fall from her lips.

"It was," he said, with a scoundrel's smile. "I do believe you're jealous of her."

"I am not!" she retorted hotly. "I was only curious."

"Well, you needn't worry. Miss Sidney is far away and is no rival for my affections. How can I begin to consider another woman when you are so near to me?"

Rosie hoped with all her heart that his remark would not be brought to a test.

There were hundreds of carriages and riders with women dressed like exotic birds in every color of the rainbow. Even little children were dressed in costumes imitating grand *caballeros* and flamenco dancers. Juan stopped often to exchange words with people in carriages and in the *casetas*. Sherry was brought out to them in tiny glasses so that they didn't have to dismount.

Señora Gómez was transported by the occasion. Rafaela thought her smile would be permanently emblazoned on her face for the rest of her life. "Never, never have I seen such a beautiful *feria*," she exclaimed again and again. Juan even went out of his way to buy her a dozen red roses from a vender. And Danny, not to be outdone, bought her another dozen.

Around two o'clock they all returned to the Herrera house for a leisurely lunch. Manuel sat with them, but Rosie noticed that he ate little and drank no wine. Though he laughed and smiled along with the group, he seemed to be in another world, concentrating on the coming *corrida*.

"Manuel is a very serious artist," explained Juan, "and though he would not show it, he is very nervous about the fight. Later tonight, at the parties, you will see a different man, full of jokes and laughing."

"It is such a dangerous profession," said Rosie. "What makes him do it?"

Juan shrugged. "People have been asking that for centuries. Why must I play the guitar, eh? Why do you paint? Why does someone fall in love?"

"Yes, why?" she asked him. He stared at her for a long moment. She was still dressed in her turquoise costume, the white rose in her hair.

"Do you love me, Rosita?" he pulled her close. She could feel her heart pounding, but could not answer.

He was about to kiss her when Manuel appeared, dressed in a white *traje de luces* trimmed with silver, and over that an intricately embroidered jacket of silver and gold. In spite of the bright flamboyance of the costume, he looked even more somber than he had at lunch. It reminded her of the portrait of Manolete.

With horror she also remembered the scene of Manolete's death so carefully reconstructed in the museum in Cordoba.

Danny had already become an enthusiastic bullfight *aficionado*. "I bet you'd just like to get up there and ride one of those bulls rodeo style," Rosie teased him.

"Not a chance. They're bred for nothing but killing. Once he bucked you off his back, he'd have a horn in your side before you had time to hear the applause. That to me is the most dangerous time for a bullfighter," Danny told Juan. "I've seen more bullfighters get it after they were down than during the pass."

"It is true," Juan agreed. "A man may get thrown in the air on the horns of the bull, but will not get hurt unless the bull gets to him on the ground."

"I don't think I'm going to like this sport at all," Rosie shuddered.

They waited outside the bullring for the bullfighters to arrive in their carriages, the colorful processions not unlike the parades earlier in the day. Everyone, still in costume, was in a very gay mood.

They had an excellent box just below that of the *presidente* of the *corrida* on the shady side of the ring. Rosie noticed that many people turned around in their seats to see who they were and whispered to each other.

Juan sat very close, his thigh pressed up against hers. She toyed for a moment with the Andalusian ruffles of his white shirt and mused that some men might look silly in that costume, but it only served to accentuate Juan's ruggedly handsome features.

"You like my shirt?" he leaned over and kissed her cheek.

"Very much," she whispered in his ear.

"*Te quiero*, Rosa. I love you," he said.

"Just for today?"

"And perhaps tomorrow, if you still look as beautiful."

Suddenly Rosie caught Rafaela's sad eyes staring at her. Had he once said these same words to her? Rosie found herself scanning the stands for a glimpse of Jane Sidney. How many promises of love had the Marqués de Arévalo sworn to keep and then broken?

The music started up grandly as a rider in a black cape, mounted on a prancing black Andalusian, galloped into the ring. The colorful procession of bullfighters and their assistants followed. So far, Rosie liked the spectacle. But the sight of the bull unnerved her. He looked every bit like an unearthly beast born and bred to kill. But there was a powerful grace and beauty about him. No wonder he was so symbolic an animal to the Spaniard.

There was also much she did not like, especially the *picadores*, even after Juan explained to her the reason for them.

The two other matadors were fighting before Manuel Herrera and they gave excellent performances. Rosie was moved by the balletic quality of their movements, with the wide sweeping motion of the cape. But since none of them came close to being gored, she was beginning to think that the element of danger was exaggerated and told Juan so.

"I shall hope you don't see a goring today," he answered simply.

Manuel's bull suddenly thundered into the ring.

Rosie was struck with terror as she thought of Manuel, someone she *knew*, having to face the huge wild animal. Before, it had seemed so impersonal—like a movie.

"I'm glad you play the guitar instead of fighting bulls," she whispered to Juan and held his hand tightly while the bull rushed across the ring to Manuel's pink and yellow *capota*. He made three dramatic passes with the *capota* swirling about his body. When he walked away from the bull, dragging the cape proudly behind him, she breathed a sigh of relief and prayed that the bull would not change his mind and charge at his back.

The crowds seemed especially pleased with his *capota* work, and Juan commented, "Manuel is in good form today. I can tell by the way he handles the *capota*. You will see a good *faena*."

But as the assistants lined the bull up for the *picador*, a dark expression crossed Juan's face and the faces of the others in the box. "He hooks," Juan told her. "Manuel will have to be careful."

Rosie felt herself tense up again with expectation as the final act of Manuel's *faena* approached. He walked up to the box and dedicated the bull to his mother and threw his hat to her in the box. Rosie saw her smile calmly and then, as Manuel turned away, clutch the hat to her breast and mutter a prayer.

The first few passes received loud *olés* from the crowd. Manuel grew bolder and inched himself even closer to the bull with small steps. "He has the control," said Juan. "Watch how he trains the bull to trust him, so they move as one. It is not unlike making love."

Manuel, his feet planted in the ground, leaned back, drawing the huge animal around him with his cape.

Their fears that the bull would hook seemed groundless until just as Manuel was finishing the last of his passes, the bull suddenly lifted his head as he neared. Manuel was tossed up into the air. There were screams. Manuel was on the ground, and the bull was barreling toward him. Señora Herrera was white. The crowd had risen to its feet. Juan kept his arm tightly around Rosie's waist. Suddenly Manuel's assistant rushed out with a cape and lured the animal away just in time.

A moment of silence passed while they waited to see if Manuel would move. He lay motionless. Not a breath in the arena was taken. Rosie clutched tightly to Juan's arm leaving nail marks.

Slowly, Manuel stood up. There were blood stains on his jacket. *"Madre de Dios,"* she heard his mother whisper.

He glanced over at her from the center of the arena as if to reassure her he was all right, picked up his red *muleta* from the ground and waved his assistants away from the bull.

"Juan, he's not going to continue to fight that bull, is he?" asked Rosie in utter astonishment.

"He would be a very bad matador if he did not," said Juan. "Unless he is dying, a matador will always get up again to fight the bull. It is a matter of honor. Of courage."

Later back at the Herrera house in Seville, Juan took Rosie into the room where Manuel was celebrating with his friends and assistants. Rafaela had declined to go in. "It is not the place for a woman. The men can be very crude," she cautioned. But Juan assured her it would be all right. "They will swear in Spanish and you don't know enough of the language to be shocked by it."

But Rosie noticed that she was the only woman in the room. Champagne was passed around. Rosie took a glass and stood very close to Juan. Manuel greeted them with a huge relaxed grin. How different a man, thought Rosie, than the somber one who had left earlier for the *corrida*. "How did you like the bullfight?" he asked her.

"I was very impressed," she said with genuine admiration. "Especially when you went back after the bull tossed you."

"I was not hurt," he shrugged.

"But your jacket . . ." She pointed to the bloodstains on his white *traje de luces*.

"That was from the bull," he laughed and held the jacket out to her. "Here, would you like to wear it?"

Juan draped it over her shoulders. She nearly collapsed under the weight. "You didn't tell me it was so heavy!"

"It is the silver," he laughed. "But sadly, it is not heavy enough to protect me from the horns of the bull!"

When the assistants began unlacing Manuel's pants, Rosie suggested to Juan that she leave. "And miss the best part of the show?" he teased her.

"Really, Juan," she protested and made for the door, but

he pulled her back and yelled something in Spanish across the room to Manuel's assistants. Two men rushed forward with the *capota* and formed a makeshift dressing room, shielding Manuel's body from Rosie's view.

"You see how ingenious we Spaniards are!" he called to her.

When he emerged, Rosie marvelled at how untypical looking he was for a bullfighter, or for her idea of a Spaniard. He had straight, sandy-colored hair and blue eyes. People said he looked like the famous El Cordobés, whose flamboyant style also resembled his.

"Where was Manuel's girlfriend?" asked Rosie later as they were climbing into the coach to go back to the fair at night. "Or doesn't he have one particular lady?"

"It is very difficult to be the girlfriend of a matador—more difficult even than to be the girlfriend of a musician. But women are very fond of Manuel. You will see tonight, there will be no lack of admirers around him."

"And will I have to fight them off you, too?"

"No, I was not the main performer today. Manuel is the hero. They will ignore me."

Rafaela's mother was too exhausted for any parties that night. She decided to stay home with Señora Herrera and watch the festivities on television.

Instead of going back to their private *caseta*, they went to a larger one, a private club that had a band and dance floor. Rosie recognized many celebrities, movie stars, politicians, international jet setters and royalty. It did not escape her that had she come to Seville alone, she would have been nothing more than Rosie Powell from Wichita. But arriving with Juan de Arévalo on one arm and Manuel Herrera on the other raised her up to the status of a minor celebrity.

When she had seen the glamorous photographs of women hanging on the arms of movie stars in magazines, she had always felt a faint twinge of envy, as though the stardust must rub off on their companions. But as more and more people crowded around them, she felt suddenly very small and insignificant. Several times women cut in between her and Juan, purposely separating them. Luckily Juan quickly found her hand again and brought her back into the conversation, but the talk was very often in a language she did not understand.

It was awkward being at his side during those moments, an appendage, unimportant but for the reflected glitter of the real celebrity. There was a poignant loneliness in it, despite the crowds, and she wished selfishly that Juan would break away from them all and take her off somewhere alone.

Up until that night, he had bestowed his almost undivided attention on her but now he was spread thin. She could tell by his broad smiles and gracious manner that he gloried in the attention, the flattery, and she knew that if she were ever to be a part of his life, that she would have to accept this social part of him, this egotistical need of his for adulation. It was part of what made him unique—what had catapulted him onto concert stages.

Danny was enjoying himself, comfortable in any surroundings, and Rafaela was drawn in by the people and excitement. Looking around at the Spanish women, Rosie decided that her sister-in-law was by far the most beautiful, and even though she had no title attached to her name, she looked more aristocratic that any of them. It occurred to Rosie that nobility was not something one necessarily inherited like a title. It was a way of looking at life. She remembered on the farm; there were even animals, chickens and horses, even cows that held themselves in such a regal way as to be named "King" or "Duchess."

So many people were coming over to their table to congratulate Manuel on the excellent bullfight, Rosie could not keep track of them all as she was introduced, but she was well aware, from the conversations, that Juan and Manuel both enjoyed reputations as international playboys. People always seemed to be reminding them of one party or another they'd all attended a week, month or a year before in places as far apart as Calcutta, Cannes or Rio. She mused that she knew people in Wichita who didn't get together that often.

The name almost slipped by her as she was being introduced to a glamorous, flaming red headed woman with a

British accent. Then it came back to her in a flash, the face from a dozen movies and magazine covers. "Rosa, I would like you to meet Jane Sidney," Juan was saying.

The Oscar-winning actress held out a heavily jeweled hand to be shaken. Rosie quickly looked at Juan to see if she could detect any reaction from him. As far as she could discern, he seemed genuinely pleased to see her.

"I had no idea you were in Spain," he told her.

"Have you ever known me to miss the exciting *feria* in Seville, my love?" she smiled at him beguilingly. Rosie felt the first uneasy pangs of jealousy.

"But I heard you were having a torrid romance in Acapulco with some director," he teased.

"Past tense, my darling. And that Acapulco sun was ruining my sensitive Anglo-Saxon skin. Do you mind if I join your little party?"

"No, not at all. Please sit down." Juan brought a chair over for her and she sat between him and Manuel.

Rosie felt miserable. Both Juan and Manuel were fawning over Jane, and other people who knew them were soon coming over to their table and saying things like, "So you two are back together again? Arévalo, I've never known you to be constant to anything but your guitar."

All of a sudden, the club felt suffocatingly crowded and full of smoke. Rosie stood up quietly so that Juan would not see her and went outdoors into the cool night. It was insane to think he would love me, she thought. I was only an entertaining little romance. I could never be as scintillating as Jane Sidney or any of the other women in there. She began to walk aimlessly under the trees and realized that the sherry had made her slightly tipsy.

"Rosie!" called out a voice behind her. It was Danny. "What are you doing alone out here at night? Are you crazy?"

"Oh, Danny, I want to go home. I don't belong here."

"You go on back in there," he said sternly.

"Those people are so different from us; I have nothing to say to them."

"Rosie, they're just *people*. There's nothing special

about them, and they're friendly as anyone in Wichita if you're friendly to them. You're just miffed because Juan's old lady friend is there, right?"

She nodded.

"Well, you go back and defend what's yours!"

"Mine? I don't *own* Juan de Arévalo. I don't think even Jane Sidney owns him."

"You're much better looking than she is."

"Sure, Danny," she laughed bitterly.

"No kidding, Rosie, when you walked in there tonight, every head turned to admire you."

"Every head but Juan's. He hasn't looked at me since Jane arrived. I'm not a fighter, Danny. I can't pick myself up out of the dust the way Manuel Herrera did this afternoon. Maybe you can find me a taxi and I'll go back to the Herrera house."

Danny took her hand and led her reluctantly back to the club. "You do, and I'll never have any respect for you, Rosie. I'll always love you, and feel a little sorry for you, but the admiration I've always had for you, for your art and your courage to come out of that thing with Chip . . . if you can't face up to this little disturbance in your life, you'll never face anything!"

His words stung her more than anything he could have said. Their love had always been based on mutual respect as well as family ties. She could not bear to lose that. Juan de Arévalo *was* a minor disturbance in comparison.

But when she walked back into the club, her timidity was replaced by rage. Jane Sidney had left Juan and was hanging adoringly on the arm of Manuel Herrera near the bar. What shocked and angered Rosie was seeing Juan de Arévalo and Rafaela sitting close together at the table, deep in conversation. He was holding her hands between his and gazing intently into her eyes.

Chapter Seven

"LOOKS LIKE WE both have something to fight about," Rosie turned to Danny.

"Come on, let's go to the bar and have a drink," he said, taking her by the hand.

Rosie's mouth fell open. "Weren't you the one who wanted *me* to defend what was mine? Aren't you going to go over there and tear that arrogant, ruthless monster apart? Danny, that's your *wife!*"

Danny was steering her to the bar. "Rosie, there is a lot more to it than that. It's very complicated. You don't know the whole story."

"It looks very simple to me. We leave for five minutes and they . . ."

"You don't know what you're saying."

"Are you too blinded by love to see the obvious!"

"Rosie! Would you let me explain?"

"Yes, explain why you would let a man steal your wife away from you before your very eyes!"

"It's not like that."

"You'd believe anything," she wheeled around and came face to face with Manuel Herrera.

"*Hola*, my pretty," he grabbed her waist and held her steady. She was aware of the tremendous power in those large hands. It was no wonder he could handle a heavy *muleta* and sword so deftly. His sandy hair was tousled and his blue eyes were sparkling with mischief. "A glass of the finest sherry," he commanded the bartender, "for the most beautiful woman in Seville."

Danny interrupted, "Rosie, I *must* talk to you and get this straightened out."

"And a glass of sherry for the most beautiful woman's brother," Manuel added. "But you both have very long, unhappy faces. Did you know that it is against the law to be unhappy at the *feria* of Seville? You could be arrested!" He clicked glasses with them in a toast. "Here is to smiles. Smiles? Eh? Ah! *Bueno*! Now you will not be arrested. Brothers and sisters, they are always arguing. My sisters— I have three—are always fighting with me. It's why I began fighting the bulls. The bullring was the one place I could go where they wouldn't follow me."

"We'll talk later," said Danny quietly to Rosie and walked away.

Rosie suddenly remembered that, moments ago, Manuel had been talking to Jane Sidney. Had Juan asked him to keep her out of the way while he intrigued with Rafaela? "What happened to Jane?" Rosie asked out of curiosity.

"Jane?"

"Jane Sidney," Rosie reminded him.

He tipped his head to one side indifferently, and glanced around. "I think she may have left, why?"

"I just thought . . . I mean, I saw her talking to you . . ."

"Jane Sidney talks to everyone. She's a very friendly girl—what you Americans call a social butterfly. Yes! A good image. She does not stay in one place for very long."

"I remember seeing a picture of her and Juan in a magazine," Rosie ventured.

"Oh, that was a big romance!" he laughed. "It lasted almost six weeks."

"That long," smiled Rosie.

"That was long for Jane, an eternity for Juan. And she had left *me* for him."

"You were her lover, too?"

He nodded.

"It doesn't sound as though you were terribly broken up that she left you for your best friend."

"Juan and I have an understanding about women. It is not something to risk a friendship over."

Rosie felt a chill, thinking that she was an interchange-able commodity that could be passed as easily between these men as a football. Now Manuel was obviously making a flirtatious play for her and did not worry that Juan would be angry with him. She looked across the room at Juan and Rafaela still lost in conversation, oblivious to everyone around them and her brother Danny at the other end of the bar, ignoring them, talking to some Americans. She was disgusted at all of them, at how little they valued them-selves, their loves and their friendships.

"There is another *caseta* down the street that has a disco band," Manuel broke into her thoughts. "It's much livelier than here. Would you like to go with me?"

She wanted to say no, that she would prefer to go back to the house, back to Cordoba or back to Wichita, but instead, she straightened her shoulders and smiled. "Yes, what a wonderful idea! I'd love to."

She did not look back over her shoulder as they walked out the door, but she hoped Juan, Rafaela and Danny were watching so they'd see she could be as unfeeling and callous as they were.

She took a deep breath of the fresh cool air of the park. "It's so pleasant out here. I almost hate to go back inside another *caseta*."

Manuel put his arm around her. "Then we won't. How does an open carriage ride sound to you?"

"Delicious."

He hailed one of the colorful horse-drawn buggies and helped her in. They leaned back and looked up at the stars between the luxuriant trees. A few carriages passed them, but the park was nearly deserted now and peaceful, but for the clip-clopping of horses on the paths.

"Did you really enjoy the bullfight today?" he asked her suddenly in a voice that had the tone of a little boy who badly wanted approval.

"Yes—much more than I thought I would. You were really magnificent, Manuel. I mean that. I never understood what bravery or courage meant until I saw you face that bull again after he'd knocked you down."

He turned her face toward him. "Your beauty does not stop with your face, Rosa. One can look into your green eyes and see your very soul. I would like to kiss you very much."

"Then why don't you?" She was thinking that Manuel was a man she could safely kiss without losing control. He was charming, handsome and most important, she felt no danger of falling in love with him. Talking to Juan made her throat go dry and gave her heart palpitations.

"I would kiss you, but you are, I'm afraid, in love with my friend, Juan."

"That's not true! I care nothing for him." And to emphasize her point, she threw her arms around Manuel's neck and pulled him to her. He did not resist, but to her surprise, his kiss did leave her a little breathless and confused. Perhaps she *could* begin to care for Manuel. And if she fell in love with him, would he treat her the same way Juan had? How soon would he be "exchanging" her for another? This whole new interplay with men was bewildering. How easy life had been with Chip. "I think I'd like to go disco dancing now," she suggested. "Imagine, disco dancing with a bullfighter!"

"Dancing and bullfighting all go back to the same origins," he said touching her cheek. "The bull was a symbol of male fertility in ancient times, and women danced on the earth to make the crops grow."

As they pulled up in front of the disco *caseta*, they saw Juan standing at the door outside, alone. "Why didn't you tell me you were leaving?" he asked Rosie.

"I didn't think it was any of your business," she said stiffly.

His eyes narrowed, and he grabbed Manuel roughly. "What were you doing with her out there?"

Manuel looked surprised and tried to calm his friend. "This is something we have never fought about before, eh?" He took Rosie's hand and led her over to Juan. "Here, you want her back?"

Rosie pulled her hand away. "I am not an object you two

can toss back and forth. I do not *belong* to either one of
you!" she said angrily.

"That is wrong!" said Juan. "You are mine. You have
no right to run off with another man."

"What a double standard you live by!" she burned with
rage. "You can do just as *you* please, but *I* must remain
faithful. What gives you the right to dictate to me?"

"I love you."

"Like you loved Jane Sidney and Rafaela?"

"Rafaela! You didn't think . . ."

"Oh, go away from me! I came here with Manuel. We
had a wonderful carriage ride. We talked about bullfighting,
we kissed, we're going dancing, and I just may be in love
with *him*." She ran into the *caseta*, but Juan grabbed her
hand and pulled her back.

"Then you do not love me?"

"No. I despise you. Leave me alone!"

He dropped her hand coldly and walked away. Manuel,
standing by, shook his head.

"Come on, Manuel," she swallowed hard to keep the
tears from erupting. "I'm in the mood to dance."

She was able to work out some of her pent-up frustration
on the dance floor with Manuel, but she was still seething
with nervous energy when the carriage brought them back
to the Herrera house in the early hours of the morning.

They had both been drinking and walked arm in arm up
to her room. "I guess everyone else is already home," she
whispered.

"And sound asleep like any sane person should be."

"Yes, sleep," she yawned. "What's that?"

"It's what you do when you are tired and there is nothing
better to do in bed." He opened the door to her room and
led her in.

"Where's the light?" she mumbled as she heard him shut
the door behind him.

"You like the light on?" he whispered, drawing her close.

She suddenly understood what he meant, and she pushed
him away. "Oh no, Manuel."

"Good, then we will keep the light off." She felt his lips on her neck as he unzipped her dress. The liquor had blurred her senses, and his caresses felt very pleasing on her tired body. She gave in for a moment and let her sensations take over. It would be fine, she knew, to have a lover like Manuel. She would not have to care for him. He would be a passionate lover even though he did not excite her as Juan had. He could be the man to make her forget Chip and Juan. Juan! She had forgotten that he was staying in that very house. Rafaela, Danny, Señora Gómez, Señora Herrera—they were *all* there.

"Manuel, this is not the place to do this."

"Nobody will hear us," he assured her.

"No, I won't," she stiffened. "Everyone is here."

He kissed her lightly and sighed. "To leave a man in such a state is criminal, but you are probably right." He backed away.

"Manuel, wait—before you go—"

"You have changed your mind?" he asked hopefully.

"No—but you still haven't shown me where the lights are."

He turned them on for her and closed the door quietly. Rosie sank down on the bed and took off her dress quickly. There was a voice in the hall. Were others just getting in, too? Had they seen Manuel leave her room? It was unmistakably Juan's voice. Her heart stopped. He and Manuel were rapidly exchanging words in Spanish. She heard Juan say, "What were you doing in there?"

And Manuel lying, "In bed, she is a dream, my friend. Much better than Jane."

Juan used angry words she didn't understand, then there was the sound of a fist making contact with flesh and a loud thud against the wall. Several doors opened down the hall.

Chapter Eight

SEÑORA HERRERA SLEEPILY asked what was going on and she heard Manuel respond, "Nothing, go back to sleep, everyone go back to sleep." Then in a quieter voice he added, "Juan—you're acting like a crazy man. She is just a woman—nothing to get crazy about!"

"You're right. Yes, you're right," mumbled Juan. "I'm sorry I hit you. I must be crazy."

"The horns of bulls have done much more damage to my body than your fists, my friend. I worry more about your hands for the guitar than your heart. Love is a very bad thing for you; you must not risk it again, or you will throw away a great career as a guitarist."

Rosie could not hear the rest of what they said for they were walking down the hall. But she couldn't help wondering what everyone else who heard that conversation was thinking.

Unable to sleep, she kept turning over in her mind the last conversation between Juan and Manuel. It was difficult to believe that Juan really loved her as he claimed, especially after he all but deserted her for Jane, then Rafaela. Was it only some sort of Spanish machismo possessiveness he felt for her? But then why would he hit his best friend? There had obviously been no fights over Jane. But Jane had gone from Manuel to Juan, not the other way around.

She pushed all thoughts of Danny and Rafaela's marriage out of her mind, for as painful as it was to think about Juan and Manuel, it was torture to consider what was happening between her brother and his wife.

Oddly, she was not offended by Manuel's lies about her. At least she knew exactly where she stood with him. There was no pretense of love. The attraction between them was purely physical. It was not poetry and music caressing her soul; Juan de Arévalo was all those things, and more. She remembered the night they had slept peacefully in each other's arms and thought how pleasant it would be to have him next to her now to hold her until she fell asleep.

Rosie's dreams were often a combination of symbolism and reality. Sometimes she saw a giant canvas and, as she added the shapes and colors, she saw them become animated into recognizable forms, often people she knew, and she would be pulled, like Alice through the Looking Glass, into her own creation.

Tonight as she drifted into sleep, the rush of wild bulls thundering toward her began as indistinct patterns of black, and gradually, as they moved, acquired horns and flared angry nostrils. She stood in a *traje de luces*, turquoise with glittering gold embroidery. Instead of letting the bull pass by her, she wrapped herself around him in a moment of terror and discovery. As the cloud of dust settled, Juan suddenly appeared, and joined her in a wild flamenco dance. His nostrils were flared like the bull's, the tilted Cordovan hat shadowing his black eyes that sparked with the same animal magnetism as the bull's. His back arched and his chin lowered, he coaxed her around his lean body as though she were a marionette and he the master who controlled the strings.

As they danced and whirled, the strings wrapped around her, binding him to her, tighter and tighter until they were stretched taut and she was no longer a dancer, but lying across his lap, his long, sensitive fingers pressing into her neck. She was his guitar.

His right hand caressed the blond wood of her body, the sensuous curves of the guitar molded themselves, as though having a life of their own, against the hard muscles of his chest and thighs. It was as though he were fashioning them for his own pleasure as he played. Pressed so tightly against him she could hear his heartbeat, she put her own heart in a steady, pulsing rhythm with his.

As he strummed the passionate chords, her whole body arched towards him, craving to become part of him. She longed to be his very soul. His fingers moved down her long neck pressing in different configurations, each chord awakening a new passion, while his other hand strummed wildly at the strings. A strange primitive music reverberated and echoed in her depths, pulsing, straining, trembling against the wooden insides for release.

As the strings were plucked in patterns of sounds she heard in her dream, her wooden shell grow soft and malleable. Now he caressed not only the strings, but every portion of her guitar body and, wherever he touched, fiery flames ignited and turned her body into flesh. He had transformed her, by the magic of his musical genius, into a living breathing woman. He was her master, and she realized with terror that with one indifferent stroke of his strong hands, she could become a mere wooden guitar again. No one would ever know what music she was capable of producing. No one would ever know what secret harmonies she held in the depths of her soul.

She must not let him stop caressing her, or the woman held captive in her wooden body would vanish forever. She stretched out arms to him, encircling his neck, pulling his head down to kiss her lips. He must know that I am a woman, she thought desperately in her dream. But he was kissing her only lightly, as though he didn't believe what she had become. With urgency, she pressed her lips with small movements, running her tongue across his sensuous lips. He was responding, she felt with relief, and he forced her mouth open with a fiery power, his own tongue now thrusting, finding hers. The rhythm of their heartbeats crescendoed. She moved against him purposefully, feeling his hardening virility. Must not let him stop now, she thought wildly.

As the wood of her guitar body became more and more the soft yielding flesh of a woman under his magic hands, she slowly found herself stirring in the strange middle area between sleep and wakefulness. She realized as she responded with a demanding urgency to her dreamlike desires, that it was more real than fantasy.

There *was* a man in bed with her!

Had Manuel come back to prove himself after all? Did he want to make his lie to Juan into reality? The mouth on hers was moving slowly down her neck—so like Juan had done that afternoon at his *palacio* in Cordoba.

But it was deathly black in the room. In Spain, there were shutter-like wooden slats that fit over the windows outside and shut out the glare of the morning sun. At night, they made a room pitch black.

The kisses that were making her body sing were like Juan's, but what would he be doing in her room at that late hour, especially after the violent scene in the hall? Hadn't he intimated that his friendship with Manuel was more important than a woman? It had to be Manuel.

"Manuel?" she whispered tentatively.

"Yes, *mi amor*." Something in the way he said those words reminded her of Juan. Manuel had never said that to her, even jokingly; Juan had called her *mi amor* many times. But why would Juan want her to think that it was Manuel?

She slid her hand up his lean throat and traced the outline of his eyebrow, down the side of his face and across his lips as he kissed her fingertips gently. With her artist's hand she knew. It was Juan.

In her basic drawing classes in art school, how often had the teacher made them go up to a still life and touch it. "You cannot draw a texture without knowing how it feels," he had said. She had gone through a period of touching everything she could, with her eyes closed, then translating it to paper without having ever used the sense of sight. That practice stood her in good stead now. The aristocratic high cheekbones and straight nose, the thick lush texture of his black hair, the wide sensuous lips with the cynical curl. There was nothing about the man lying next to her that was anything like the bullfighter, Manuel.

She felt the anger welling like a violent hurricane within her chest. Why was he playing this charade with her? It could only be to test Manuel's lie. If she were to respond as a lover, then there could be no doubt left in his mind that Manuel had made passionate love to her as he had said in the hall.

She wondered how long he had been there—how he had so perfectly melted into her dream. Did he think she was awake? What actually had she done?

Rosie was furious.

Why couldn't he have simply confronted her in the morning? Why did he have to play such a deviously cruel trick? With a sudden obstinacy, she whispered, "Manuel, why have you come back to me tonight?" She kissed the hollow of his neck, nuzzling against him as she spoke.

"I wanted you again. I want to make love to you again and again."

This made her even angrier. There was no question now. He *was* trying to trick her.

"But I'm very tired now."

"Did I tire you out?"

"Yes. You were wonderful, Manuel," she decided to add a barb. "The most wonderful lover I have ever had."

She could feel Juan stiffen next to her, and she smiled secretly in the dark. She would give him back his own medicine.

"But you must go now, Manuel, I'm so very tired and I'll want to see more of the *feria* tomorrow."

"I want you," he whispered in a husky voice, pulling her under him. He ran his hands forcefully down her sides, pressing her tightly against him. She squirmed to free herself, but he held her there, under his powerful lean body. "And you want me. We'll make it better than before, Rosa." The weight of his long muscled legs was forcing hers apart, she realized with alarm.

"No, not again tonight."

"You will love it even more." He arched his back, freeing her breasts, and he cupped them in his strong hands, playing with sensitive fingers. She felt as though she were a guitar again, transformed by his touch. "Do you love it, Rosa? Tell me, tell me how you love it. I can feel your heartbeat."

She felt herself grow weak and yielding, unable to protest.

"Tell me how you love it."

She could only give a slight moan, throwing her head back against the pillow, giving herself to the surges of passion that racked her slender body.

"Tell me, Rosa." It was no longer his long fingers, but his lips, playing, teasing, for his hands were now moving down to more sensitive areas.

Never before had she felt such fiery longings, as though her body were illuminated with molten white heat, tinged with scarlet wherever he touched.

With Chip, sex had been only something to withhold through high school, portioning out parts of the body to be petted at certain intervals in their long relationship during awkward explorations in the back seat of his car.

After they were formally engaged, she had felt that it was okay to "go all the way" since they would be married soon. And even though the wedding date kept being put off for one reason or another, the sex continued, never inspired, always slightly awkward in the back seat sort of way. It was something she reluctantly gave in to because *he* wanted it, nothing she craved, nothing her whole being cried out for. And she had never been curious about his body, never aggressively interested in catering to his needs.

The utter blackness of the room and knowing that Juan was convinced she thought he was Manuel gave her an uncharacteristic boldness she never knew she possessed.

It was not enough to receive what Juan was giving her; she wanted to return it, paint his body with the same swirls of scarlet and vermillion.

But how? She knew so little. Why hadn't she ever picked up some of those books her friends in art school used to secretly devour? What could she do to make him as wildly passionate as she felt?

Her inhibitions melted away as his musician's hands pressed the soft inside of her thighs. She reached down her hands and, thinking of the tips of her fingers as sable tips of paint brushes, she began to design her passion in patterns of searing blue-white light.

She heard him moan and throw back his head. "Rosa, Rosa . . ." Improvise, improvise, she told herself. It's not necessary to be able to reproduce every color, each note of the *concierto*. One can paint and create music as one feels. She ran her lips across his chest, using them as she would a palate knife for texture. If her own nipples were sensitive, then so would his be.

Whatever she attempted seemed to increase his own determination to bring her to ecstasy. There were no longer set patterns to the way they moved together. Everything was improvisation; nothing was to be drawn the way it should be. This was a new art form that changed with the whim of a second, that they created together as the passionate souls of two artists meshed into one.

Like passionate flamenco dancers who never tired, circling, finding new rhythms to match their violent heartbeats, they arched their backs and swirled around each other, their passion like the flaming red *muleta* of the matador wrapping around them, plunging them deeper into their raging artists' souls.

When Rosie opened her eyes, she saw that the room had a blue grey tint. Slender shafts of light filtered through the shutters. There was the hollow feeling in the pit of her stomach that tells the body it is morning. She turned her head and saw Juan's sharply defined profile on the pillow next to her, his lips slightly parted, his eyes closed.

She freed her stiff right arm which was pinned under him and the movement stirred him. His arm, which was under her neck, tightened around her shoulder and pulled her close. He kissed her forehead, then opened his eyes.

"Are you surprised to find *me* here?"

"No," she whispered. "I knew it was you all along."

His upper lip curled with disbelief.

"You did?"

"Juan!" she stammered. "Of course I knew!"

"It was so dark I could barely find your bed. How could you have known? Don't lie to me."

"Juan—don't be ridiculous. I would never have made love if I hadn't known it was you."

"Don't give me that, Rosa. You made love to Manuel earlier."

"I've never made love to Manuel!"

"Manuel doesn't lie to me."

"But you think *I* would?"

"What else can I think? You called Manuel's name, didn't you?"

"That was just because you made me so mad by coming in here and trying to deceive me. I wanted you to have a taste of your own medicine."

"You're trying to cover. You thought I was Manuel and wanted another taste of what he gave you."

"Juan! You're impossible. Why won't you believe me?"

He studied her in the indistinct light. "After what you did at the *caseta*, running off with Manuel. Why should I believe you? You wanted me to think you were inexperienced. But I learned differently last night. You made passionate love with more sophistication than any woman I've ever known. You have things in your repertoire, *mi querida*, that other women have not yet begun to dream of. You've been lying to me all along."

She was so appalled she could hardly speak. He had taken a beautiful spiritual experience, a totally unexpected, spontaneous outpouring of passion and turned it into a circus sideshow. "And I suppose you had nothing better to do tonight, having failed to win Rafaela away from Danny with all your considerable charm and sex appeal. You had to play silly games with me."

"You do not know what you're saying," his eyes flashed dangerously. "Don't ever say that about Rafaela!"

"Any man who would try to seduce a girl by disguising himself as another man would be unscrupulous enough to go after another man's wife. Did you think I wouldn't want you as you were? Well, you were right. I *did* think you were Manuel!" She couldn't believe the treacherous words

as they tumbled helter-skelter from her mouth, but they
continued as though they had a life of their own. She knew
only that she wanted to hurt him, wound him badly where
he was most vulnerable. "Do you think if I had known it
was you, I would have let you stay in my bed? I loathe you.
I despise you! Manuel was a much better lover. He knows
things *you* could never even imagine. And you fancy yourself such a genius. You may be a guitar virtuoso, but you
are an amateur when it comes to a woman's body."

"So why did you let me continue?" he said, his dark
eyes narrowing. She saw that she had wounded him, but
it gave her no pleasure. She wanted to reach out, tell him
how precious every moment had been and erase all the
words, but every horrible syllable was now indelibly
printed on his mind.

"I . . . I . . ."

"You were curious. Is that it?"

"Juan," she pleaded, but he was already putting on his
clothes.

He turned and looked at her with dark eyes of loathing.
"For awhile, Rosa, I thought . . ." He paused and stared at
her. "But it was my mistake. A bad mistake. It's all been
a very bad mistake."

Before she could say another word, he had crossed the
room and was out the door.

She listened to his footsteps down the long hall and
turned her face to the pillow, stifling the sobs that came
from her silent anguished depths.

Chapter Nine

THE NEXT MORNING Danny told her that Juan had left Seville early that morning for London to do a concert. "When will he return?" she asked.

"He didn't say."

"Are we going back to Cordoba today?"

Danny nodded. "We have a lot of things to discuss; you, me, Rafaela and her mother."

"Danny, I feel like I'm disrupting things here. Maybe I should just travel alone for awhile."

"Rosie, come back to Cordoba now. Once we explain matters to you, it will be easier. I was wrong. I should have insisted you know everything from the outset. Now, it may be too late."

There was a long silence in the car until they were on the highway out of town. It seemed to Rosie that they were all waiting to divulge their secret until the city was no longer there to eavesdrop. She could not imagine what was so difficult to discuss but knew it revolved around Juan de Arévalo.

"Perhaps you should begin," Danny told Rafaela, breaking the silence.

"No, I think it is for my mother to begin the story," she said slowly. "Can you tell it, Mamá?"

Señora Gómez nodded. "The years heal over many wounds, especially the worst ones, those of pride. I will tell you, Rosa, that when I was younger than you, a girl of fifteen, I was very poor. You cannot imagine how poor are the Spanish peasants. My family lived in a cave, one room for many children who were thin and ill fed. My mother died young in childbirth and my father could barely feed us. But we were given an overabundance of love and pride that was way beyond our station in life.

"As soon as we were old enough, we either married or left to find work or both. I found a job in a small restaurant in a village near the Arévalo vineyards. Since I had no shoes and only one dress, they kept me in the back to wash dishes, mop the floors and feed the chickens. I was very lonely without my sisters, brothers and my father, even though the people who owned the restaurant were kind to me and gave me my own small room in back of the restaurant.

"One day some young men arrived in a yellow motorcar. They were dressed in the most magnificent clothes I had ever seen. Now looking back it was probably nothing more than most wealthy people wear, but then I was amazed—white pressed shirts, pants with creases and without holes. I stood in the doorway, gaping at them, as though they were exotic animals in a zoo. One of them smiled at me—he was very handsome, beautiful, sympathetic dark eyes, a narrow face and very white teeth—I will never forget that look. He said, '*Hola*, a girl dressed in rags and the face of a princess.'"

"At that, they all turned around and agreed that I indeed looked more elegant in my old clothes than any real princess they had ever known. From then on, whenever they stopped at the restaurant, they asked for 'the princess' to wait on them."

"When the marqués met my mother," Rosie cut in, "he was only eighteen years old, and even though he had been married a year, he had never been in love."

Señora Gómez picked up the narrative again. "He was a very sensitive boy. We would sit under the olive trees at night and he would read to me the poetry he'd written or play the guitar—not nearly as well as Juan does now, but he was very good. If he had studied, he might have also done concerts; he had a wonderful voice. Everyday he brought me a present—something very nice just to show he had been thinking of me—a bouquet of rosebuds, a bag of chocolates. I was the only person in the world, he claimed, who had ever really listened to him. Listen? Oh, I worshipped him like a god and I prayed to Jesus to forgive me for loving a man so very much. When I . . .," her voice faltered for a moment, "when we . . . conceived our baby, I knew it was a sin, but something in me said that when there was so much love between two people, it could not be wrong.

"He wanted to buy me a house, clothes, all the things to provide for the baby. Part of me wanted to accept, but the other told me that accepting the gifts would make me officially his mistress. When one is sixteen years old, these reasonings seem very clear, so I took nothing from him. But when my time came closer, I began to worry about how I would provide for the child. For most of my life I had known nothing but gnawing hunger. I wanted better for my child.

"When it was a boy, the marqués was overcome with joy, and since he knew that he would never have any children with his wife, he asked my permission to let him and his wife adopt the baby legally. At first, I refused. I knew what I had done was a sin, but to give up one's own child was even worse. And yet, I had nothing to offer the child. I could have accepted the gifts of money from the marqués, but I had seen other mothers grow old and ugly—forgotten as mistresses by the men who had once adored them. At least if my child were legally adopted by his natural father, he would never know hunger. He would have a chance in life to rise out of the poverty I was born into. And most important, I knew that he would have his father's love . . ."

All at once Rosie understood. "Then Juan de Arévalo is actually your son!"

Señora Gómez nodded.

"And Rafaela?"

"She was born a few years later. I had finally accepted a small loan to buy a *bodega* in Cordoba so that I could be near Juan and watch him grow up. It soon became clear that the marquesa wanted nothing to do with him. I think she always suspected that he was her husband's natural child. The resemblance was too striking. His father brought him often to the *bodega*, but he was not told who I was. I could not hug and kiss him and cradle him in my arms. It was agony for me. Then when Rafaela was born, he wanted to adopt her too, but I refused. A second time, I could not lose a baby of mine.

"And by this time, the *bodega* was doing well. I have a talent for cooking and the news of good food travels very fast in a town like Cordoba.

"Those first years when Rafaela was little, he used to bring Juan over to play with his sister. We would all laugh together. Rafaela knew who her father was, but Juan was not told what me and Rafaela were to him.

"Then, the marquesa died. I thought naturally—well, I *dared* to hope that he would marry me, that we could raise our children together. It was not his money I wanted. I had more than enough from the *bodega*—more than I'd ever had in my life. It seemed like a fortune. I had paid him back his loan long ago and I never accepted a *peseta* from him—only gifts for Rafaela, his daughter. To be a grand marquesa was not my dream. I only wanted to be the wife of the man I loved, to raise our children. . . ," her voice broke off.

Rafaela continued. "Family pride ran too thick in his veins. The old aristocracy of Spain. My father was a coward."

"You can look back and say that, Rafaela," Señora Gómez interrupted quickly, "but in those days it was unthinkable. Even now, it is hardly ever done that a man marries below his station."

Rafaela sighed, "After all these years, she still defends him. But when he would not marry her, she refused to ever see him again. My mother is very religious. She could not go on forever, knowing he was free to marry, and continue living in sin."

"One can forgive oneself the innocence of youth for only so long," added the Señora softly.

"But what did the marqués do?" asked Rosie.

"He was very brokenhearted. He wanted everything to

continue as before. He begged and pleaded with my mother, promised that he would never marry another woman—but she held her ground."

"There has never been another man in my life," said the Señora softly, "although I have had many proposals of marriage since. I truly believe that there is only one love inside a woman. Perhaps he believed that too because he never remarried. But I did not see him again. He stayed away from Cordoba. Juan was shuttled off to boarding schools and later, music conservatories. In the summer he vacationed with his father on Capri or Mallorca. In the winter he skied in Switzerland.

"Then, when he was eighteen, he attended a special school for flamenco guitar here in Cordoba. By that time, I had my restaurant and it was very popular—as you may have noticed—with young people. He would come in with a gang of his friends from the school, rowdy and rude, sometimes. I thought by then that his father had told him who his real mother was, and I was very upset at how indifferent he was to me and Rafaela. She was sixteen at the time, a difficult age, and wanted a brother very badly, someone older to trust and talk to, to confide in—I guess like you and Danny. But he ignored her. Now I know that he was ignorant, but then I thought he was only cruel, ashamed of us and flaunting it maliciously in our faces. This went on for many years. Whenever he was in Cordoba he came to the Conejo Blanco. Never once did he ever have a kind word."

"Then last summer," said Rafaela, "just before Danny arrived, the marqués died. On his deathbed he told Juan everything—that mama was the only woman he had ever loved. He left us a lot of money in his will and all the Arévalo vineyards. In his will he said he wanted my mother to have them because it was near where they first met. But we would not accept."

"I did not accept anything from him while he was alive," said the Señora, "I would not take a guilt offering from the grave. Juan came to us; he apologized for treating us rudely in the past. But I could not believe that he did not know all those years. I felt that now, when he was suddenly without any family, he had come to find solace. Rafaela and I turned him away." Rosie saw the Señora had tears in her eyes.

"I'm beginning to understand, now—why this whole trip to Seville for the *feria*. He wanted to make it up to you. Prove his sincerity! Why, the marqués never had the courage to do what he has done."

"Juan is a better man than his father," said Rafaela.

"He is living in different times," said the Señora.

Rosie sighed and looked helplessly at Danny. "Did you know all this?"

"Rafaela told me the entire story after I mentioned meeting Juan de Arévalo on the road."

"But why didn't you tell *me* then? Think of the grief it would have saved!"

"I asked him not to," explained Rafaela.

"But why?"

"She was afraid Danny's sister would not like her if she knew the truth about her parents," said the Señora.

"Oh, Rafaela! That's crazy! You and your mother are wonderful people. I don't give a hoot where you came from or what your social status is. Maybe that's just coming from Kansas, the way Danny and I were raised. It's what people *make* of themselves that counts. Look at Juan. It doesn't make any difference that he was born with a title and lands, because he has studied hard to be a concert guitarist. That's what is important about him, and that he is a good person!" She now realized how badly she'd misinterpreted his talking to Rafaela the night before. It was the first time in their lives that Juan and Rafaela had sat down and talked as brother and sister. No wonder Danny insisted on leaving them alone. He, of all people, knew how important it was for a brother and sister to be friends. "Oh, but I really messed things up last night! And Juan, I thought he . . . and he thinks *I* care nothing for him. Danny, I've got to call him and tell him it was all a mistake!"

Chapter Ten

As soon as they reached Cordoba, Rosie placed a long distance call to Juan's hotel in London. He hadn't arrived yet, so she left a message. When he hadn't returned her call a few days later, she called again and left another message. The next day a postcard arrived addressed to Señora Gómez, "London is cold and foggy. The concert rehearsals have begun. I think of you and Rafaela often and send you a bouquet of thoughts. My regards to Danny. Love, Juan."

Rosie bit her lower lip. He must have received her messages, and by the postcard demonstrated that he did not care to return them. She was not even worth mentioning.

Rafaela offered to write him a letter and explain. "Thank you," said Rosie, "but I deserve his scorn. I was ready to think the worst of him. I told him I despised him and ran off with his best friend. I behaved abominably, childishly. He has every right not to want to see me again."

Though she would never admit it, she was secretly relieved that Juan wanted nothing more to do with her. The strength of her feelings for him had been frightening. Everything had happened too fast. She had been swept away, unable to think clearly, and at the first test of her love, she became engulfed in a jealous rage simply because he was talking to an ex-girlfriend in a friendly fashion. It had been a romance without solid foundation, much too explosive to last. Now perhaps, time and distance would heal all the wounds, make it easy to forget.

But she was unable to forget him easily. Sometimes, as she painted, she found herself thinking about him and then she would splash violent colors on the canvas, make wide sweeps with her paintbrush or palate knife. She became impatient with the usual calm, studied style and her canvases began to reflect the emotional turmoil she was experiencing.

And while she filled her personal sketchbooks with dozens of portraits of Juan, which often took on a deeply erotic tone, she refused to actually paint his face and body into her paintings. Somehow that represented defeat to her and much too public a display of her emotions. Instead, like the symbols from her dream, he took the form of a wild bull, nostrils flared in anger, black muscles rippling with power and fury. There were long fingered hands plucking the trembling strings of a flamenco guitar while the female shaped instrument poured forth the riotous profusion of Andalusian flowers: the reds, purples and scarlets of her dizzying passion.

She painted for hours, setting up her easel out-of-doors, in a typically Cordoban *calleja*, walls laden with pots of flowers, or she would go to the old Roman bullring, the Corredera Plaza. So possessed was she that sometimes she stayed out after dark and would have to wend her way home through unfamiliar streets. But she no longer felt any panic. The Cordovans were beginning to know her. They had taken her into their hearts, softly seducing her with their warm smiles, as they had her brother Danny. The legend of her dancing the flamenco and going to the *feria* in Seville with the Marquis de Arévalo preceded her wherever she went in the small town, especially in the old picturesque quarter where the Señora's restaurant was.

The Cordovans, unlike the people of Wichita, seemed to understand what she was trying to say in her paintings, and they began to talk of the American artist with the Andalusian soul. It did not matter to them that she painted the Almodovar Gate in a glittering rainbow of colors, reflecting in the shallow pool below. They did not need to be told why she chose those colors.

Of course, they did not know that it was the agony of her situation with Juan that provoked her strong response, but they did not question her need to express herself in that way. They seemed to delight in posing for her, and she incorporated many of the faces of these people she was learning to love. The old woman who sold flowers in the Corredera Plaza had a face as intricately lined as the stones of the ancient Roman walls, and her skin was the same weather-beaten brown. "You make my face as large as the arches," she said one day to Rosie with a black-toothed smile, "but I like it very much. And I like very much the way you make the arches into the sides of guitars. You can hear the *canto* flamenco in your work, *Señorita*; you can smell the fragrance of jasmine."

It was one day at the Great Mosque that she suddenly understood the phallic symbolism of the sensuous Moorish archways and began to incorporate them into her work. At night her dreams had become more vividly erotic, detailing the extravagant night of love she had shared in the hidden darkness of the Seville room. She would lie awake in the evening, the painful longing pulsing through her, aching for the release that only Juan de Arévalo could give her. She would trace imaginary outlines of his lean body with her fingertips and felt him do the same to her. In her dreams were the pounding, sensual rhythms of the flamenco, and sometimes only his dark, heavy-lidded eyes looking down at her in a way that made her feel naked and vulnerable as licking flames of passion enveloped them in a fiery storm.

In one recurring dream, he swooped down out of the clouds like a powerful eagle and lifted her up, the two of them soaring into the night sky, arms and legs wrapped tightly around each other while they shed their human skins and became one with the universe.

When she awoke in the morning, there was always that quiet moment of desolation, the harsh realization that he was not beside her, that it had all been the exotic wanderings of her own imagination. In reality Juan was in London, perhaps even with the flaming-haired beauty, Jane Sidney. And she, Rosie, was alone.

At that moment she would pull her secret sketchbook from between the mattresses of her bed and try to put down as much of the dreams as she could remember, longing to have the nerve to paint them, but knowing how shocked Danny, Rafaela and her mother would be.

She was a little shocked at herself. Never before had she had such dangerously erotic thoughts about a man. She was amazed that she could recall so much visually even though they had lain in the dark. It was her own genius and splendid artistic training that enabled her to record those most intimate of moments, places of forbidden pleasure that had made her so vitally alive.

But where was the line between raw sexual desire and love? The intoxicating moments she dreamed about, relived breathlessly, were all things she had been taught were not for a decent girl's mind. She began to wish desperately that she had never experienced that night of mysteriously disturbing passion. Before, she might have been able to dismiss the thought of Juan as a flirtation. Now, it was impossible to ever forget him.

And yet those fevered hours with Juan seemed only the most beautiful outpourings of her love. They were, in fact, glowing expressions of that very love. Every canvas she painted was covered with the explosive patterns of it, every color tinted with it. Even her love of Cordoba was infused with her violent, bewildering love for Juan.

There were terrible moments as well as the intensely creative ones, when she wept uncontrollably into her pillow after everyone else had gone to bed—days when she lost her appetite and could not eat, so filled were her insides with painful longing for him.

One morning Rafaela came up to the roof to talk to her while she painted. She had found the roof a peaceful place on which to paint with its expansive view of the red tiled rooftops and beyond, over the Guadalquivir River, the calm beige hills of olive trees.

"Rosie," began Rafaela slowly. "So beautiful are your paintings. Danny had told me, but I did not know. They have an effect on me—how can I say. It doesn't need explanation, your work, it goes direct, like music, to the heart."

Rosie felt her heart jump at hearing her work referred

to in the same terms used to describe Juan's art.

"I think it is the music, perhaps the music of my brother Juan that inspires such creations, no?"

Rosie nodded reluctantly. She had not confided her feelings to anyone. But with Rafaela she was suddenly at ease. She *wanted* to talk. "Rafaela, I don't know what to do. This is all new to me. I have never felt this way about anyone, not even the man I was engaged to all those years."

"My mother says that those feelings come only once in a lifetime and I think she is right. I felt that way the very first time I saw Danny." Rafaela leaned back on her elbows and tilted her oval face to the sun, letting her black tresses fall loosely behind her. "How I envy you—to have your talent."

"How can you envy me? I would rather have Juan than any talent! What good does it do me?"

Rafaela sighed. "But to be able to make such beautiful things from your feelings. To translate. You see, when I was young I had so much pain because of my family. But I never had a way to get it out of me. It all built up inside then burst out in fits of anger. My mother, when she feels things, she goes to the kitchen and cooks. She makes the most wonderful dishes when her emotion is in the food. It is what I can see in your work, Rosa. What are you going to do with all these paintings?"

Rosie shrugged. "I just keep working because I have to, as though it were driving me by its own force. I don't think about a painting after I've done it. It's the act of doing it that satisfies the need. I suppose it is a little like being addicted to a drug."

"But don't you want to have an art show or something? I know you don't want us to hang them in the restaurant; you say you would be embarrassed. But you cannot keep them forever hidden from the world, letting only me and my mother and Danny see them."

Rosie stood back from her painting and squinted at it. "I don't have any idea where one even goes to have an exhibit. Who you'd talk to. And what makes you think anyone would buy one of these paintings? They're so *personal*."

"The Countess!" Rafaela sat up and clapped her hands together.

"Who?"

"You know the woman who paints her fingernails green. She has a villa near here, but she travels so often she rarely uses it. It is said that she has a sunken marble tub that fits ten people! Oh, such wicked talk!" she giggled. "You must have seen her. She comes in here almost every night when she is in Cordoba. She swears that my mother is the best cook in the world. She always wants my mother to cater a party for her friends at the villa, but my mother refuses."

"I would think she would enjoy catering," said Rosie.

"No, she cooks only in her own kitchen, and it is no longer for money that my mother cooks. She enjoys her guests here like they were part of her family. To cater a party would seem too coldly professional for her. But the Countess knows everyone everywhere. I'm sure if we showed her your work, she would know a gallery or a dealer or somebody who could help you get established."

That night the Countess arrived with three handsome men who looked young enough to be her sons, but who obviously were not. She had skin tanned as cordovan leather, but it had been pulled back over her cheekbones surgically to diminish her age, which Rosie guessed to be about fifty. She was wearing blue fingernails and eyeshadow and a dress to match, sparkling jewels on every finger, but no bracelets or necklaces. In spite of her bizarre appearance, there was an underlying warmth about the eccentric woman.

She gasped when Rosie began to show her the canvasses. "But this work is simply divine, my dear! Ravishing! How you have captured the Spaniards. You're from Kansas, you say? Oh, yes. Certainly. Your darling dear brother, Rafaela's husband. I've been to the states many times, but regretfully I've never been to Kansas, though I understand it's perfectly charming. So *rural*. Weren't you the lovely blond child riding on the back of Juan de Arévalo's horse at the *feria*? Of course, you were! Everyone was talking about it for days afterwards. He seemed quite smitten with you. What a gorgeous man he is—ah, if I were a little younger myself, not that I'm out of my prime, not yet, darlings," she laughed. She let one of her young men light a cigarette, and she touched his hand intimately.

She went carefully from one painting to the next as she talked, her eyes widening as she stood back and surveyed. "First-class work, my dear," she pronounced, tapping her cigarette holder for emphasis. "You should have the best representation in Spain, perhaps in Europe. Tomorrow morning I shall call my friend Calderón in Madrid. She's an agent. Hard nosed, my precious, but don't let that bother you too much. She will be enchanted with your work, I assure you. You mustn't let her bully you."

Rosie was so excited she could barely get to sleep that night. When she did, her dreams for the first time in weeks were not resplendent with erotic fantasies of Juan de Arévalo. They were filled instead with her paintings, and she wandered among them as though in a gallery.

It was a heady dream, filled with visions of glory and fame. But in her waking moments she realized that coupled with her desire for fame and fortune was a desire to rise to Juan's level of artistry. Even if he despised her, at least he would have to treat her as an equal. And if his opinion of her were better, if he could learn to respect her as an artist, perhaps then he would . . .

She didn't dare hope.

Chapter Eleven

A WEEK LATER the Countess appeared at the Conejo Blanco again. With her this time was a severe woman with salt and pepper hair pulled tightly back. Rosie thought she had never seen a face with so many harsh angles. The small grey eyes appeared to her as pieces of steel. Señora Calderón pursed her thin lips together and regarded Rosie's paintings silently. Rosie's palms grew damp as she nervously awaited the opinion of the agent. Her future as an artist hung by a thread.

The Condesa babbled gaily, effusing about the originality of the work. "What did I tell you, darling Calderón! Do *I* not have a good eye for talent? Have you ever seen color splashed together on a canvas with such absolutely devastating effect?"

Señora Calderón remained silent, her thin arms folded quietly across her chest.

"Well, don't leave us in suspense, dear Calderón. We're all dying to hear what you think. The poor girl is going to fall over in a dead faint if you don't speak."

Señora Calderón turned her steely eyes on the Countess. "I do not make rush judgements," she said simply and continued to regard Rosie's work. She stood before some paintings longer than others, narrowing her eyes, puckering her thin lips. Finally, she walked over to Rosie and said, "Come, we shall talk."

The Countess laughed gaily. "I *knew* you would be thrilled!"

Rosie thought that "thrilled" was an odd way to describe Señora Calderón's reaction to her work. Never had she seen someone appear so totally indifferent to her paintings. People usually liked them immensely or hated them.

They went back into the restaurant and Señora Calderón purposely selected a table for two. "We have private matters to discuss," she waved Rosie's family and the downcast Countess away.

"Your paintings have originality and they have an emotional depth that is extraordinary for so young an artist," she began, carefully weighing her words. "I suspect, Señorita Powell, that it comes from some inner turmoil that you have unleashed onto your canvasses. I have often seen this in an artist. The passions will drive an artist to create in ways he never dreamed before. But that can also be dangerous."

"Did you like the work?" Rosie finally got up the nerve to venture.

"Whether I like it personally or not is of no concern to you," she said curtly. "It is whether I can sell it or not. And I believe that I can. Like anything else, art is a marketable commodity. You artists like to think of yourselves as lofty deities in touch with the muses. It never occurs to you that you produce a product, and only that. Some people produce shovels, some people produce great works of art. And unless you are an artist who is independently wealthy, like the Marqués de Arévalo, you must concern yourself with the diminishing value of the *peseta*—or dollar, in your terms."

Rosie wondered why she had used the Marqués de Arévalo as an example. Was it only coincidence, or had the Countess told her about them? What Señora Calderón was saying to her had a deeply disturbing effect; she had never considered her work, even at the advertising agency, in the same category as a shovel.

"For my part, I would prefer to sell shovels. One can count on deadlines, so many workers working at such and such an amount per hour. There are no variables. With artists, one must worry about the temperamental fits of depression and fits of elation."

"Why don't you sell shovels then?" asked Rosie a little testily.

Señora Calderón cracked a hard smile. "Because, señorita, art is what I know best. I spent three years at the Beaux Arts in Paris, and I have been to every major and minor museum in the world. I go to the openings of every show; I watch the catalogues meticulously. I have built a fortune on being able to recognize new talent and promoting it. There is not another agent in Europe who can make an artist more successful."

"Are you saying you are interested in handling my work?" Rosie quickly resumed her visions of fame and glory.

"I am very careful about the artists I choose to handle. Women, in the past, although some have shown great genius, have been risky clients. The liberation movement may be changing that now, I don't know. Women will produce a great number of paintings, then they are seduced by the old myths of love and marriage. They begin to defer everything to their husbands and all their creative genius is repressed. A few have been able to continue with great works after marriage, but most begin to forget about deadlines and obligations. I will not tolerate that. An artist must produce a great volume of work at first. Later, you can taper off as the value goes up.

"Your work shows me promise. There are about ten paintings in that group that I could put into a show right now and they would sell very well. But the rest lack direction. Let me show you exactly what I mean."

Señora Calderón first took the best of Rosie's work and explained exactly what was good about it, then she moved to the others and detailed the faults. Rosie knew, after four years of art school, that she had never had a more comprehensive, intelligent critique and noted the suggestions carefully. Any aversion to Señora Calderón's unemotional, pragmatic style quickly faded away in her admiration for the agent's perceptive eye.

"I must have at least thirty paintings of the finest quality you are capable of producing. There are already ten. You must give me twenty more within eight weeks. Can you do it?"

"Oh yes!" said Rosie enthusiastically.

"Good. Then I shall book the gallery in Madrid and begin the advance publicity. I shall send my photographer down here and you must provide me with some biographical material. Are you still having the affair with the Marqués de Arévalo?"

Rosie flushed scarlet and stammered. "What does that have to do with anything?"

"Publicity. It is always good publicity in this business to link an artist with an already established celebrity."

"Well, he and I, we're not exactly . . ."

"Pity. There is such a good tie-in with the themes in your paintings. The guitars and dancers, all that. Well, perhaps we can persuade him to take you out on the town and we'll plant some paparrazzi at Horcher's Restaurant. You did leave on good terms, didn't you?"

"No . . . he . . . I doubt if he would do that for me."

"Well, I shall speak to the Countess. She knows everyone. She collects celebrities like some people collect stamps. We'll think of something for you, though it is a shame about Arévalo. He is scheduled to do a recital in Madrid at about the same time as I plan to open your exhibit. The timing would be splendid—for you both. It's always easier to generate excitement about an artist when there is some romantic interest. You would be amazed at the amount of free publicity. 'So and so seen at Tour d'Argent with latest beau, so and so, who is opening tonight at the Olympia.' You know, that sort of thing. This kind of talk bothers you?" She noticed Rosie's bewildered expression.

"Don't think Francisco Goya and Michelangelo didn't cultivate the right people to promote their work," she continued. "Why must you artists persist in having such lofty, unrealistic visions of yourselves?" she asked with a weary sigh. "I shall send you the contracts in the mail. Have your attorney look them over, then return them if all the terms are agreeable. I want you to read paragraph number six very carefully. If you do not meet a deadline for a gallery opening for any reason other than illness or death—your own—then our contract is dissolved. I refuse to put up with any silly artistic nonsense in my artists."

Chapter Twelve

"I ALWAYS KNEW you were a genius!" Danny hugged her after Señora Calderón and the Countess left. Señora Gómez brought out a bottle of her best sherry to celebrate.

Rosie was still in a state of shock. "She talked about lawyers and contracts and publicity. And she wants twenty more paintings in eight weeks. I'm not sure I can do it. She wants originality. How many times can one be original?"

"You will do it," said Rafaela. "That's all there is to it. You must not work in the restaurant anymore. You need a studio so you can work at night. Danny, we must convert the back storeroom into a studio."

"Please, don't go to any trouble. I prefer working outside under natural light. I will simply get up at the crack of dawn and work all day long."

"You must not tire yourself," warned the Señora with concern. "Your health is just as important as your success."

The first canvas she began after Señora Calderón's visit terrified Rosie. For the first few moments, she stared at the empty white rectangle of space, wondering how she would fill it. For the last several weeks since Juan's abrupt departure from Seville, there had been no question about what to put down.

The paintbrushes, like excited extensions of her own fingers, flew over the surface, spilling out her turbulant emotions.

But that anguish seemed less severe now since Señora Calderón's visit. Rosie wondered frantically if without pain, one could create great works of art.

She pulled out one of her secret sketchbooks and flipped

to a page where she had imagined a pastoral scene of her and Juan lying naked under a maple tree, his guitar leaning up against the tree beside them. It had been her favorite sketch, one that always calmed her when she felt in danger of losing her equilibrium. It was a sketch she had always dreamed of turning into a painting, filling it with wild flowers and lush green hills and pink clouds floating on a cobalt blue sky. She realized as she stared at the empty white canvas that it was this sketch she longed to paint, that she *must* paint, regardless of what Rafaela, her mother, or anyone thought.

After all, the two lovers in the painting could be anyone, the way their heads were turned. As she painted, she felt herself slip into the warm tranquility of the scene, Juan de Arévalo's strong arms wrapped securely around her. Rosie could feel her own skin tingle with anticipation as she smoothed the silky colors onto the canvas. There were cool green vines winding around their ankles and flowers: golden-orange like poppies, pillows of white jasmine under their heads as they kissed, their heady fragrance mingling with the perfume of their bodies.

Juan's strong hands were lifting her above the damp cool grass and onto his warm skin, and wherever he kissed her, wildflowers blossomed and bursting velvet petals cascaded down into the rushing stream below.

As Rosie painted, she forgot that she was on a roof in Cordoba. Only the painting had life; only the painting was real. It was where she wanted so desperately to be, in her crying need for Juan. As long as she needed and loved him, she would never have to worry about how she would fill her canvasses. He was the star of all her dreams, the prime moving force of her creativity.

The painting was nearing completion, that exhausting critical time when an artist cannot bear to paint another stroke for fear that it will ruin the perfect unity that exists, when she was aware that someone stood behind her watching.

"It brings tears to my eyes, Rosa," said Rafaela, her

voice cracking with emotion. "This is the most beautiful painting so far. Why have you always before been afraid to paint Juan in your pictures?"

"He is always in my paintings," she said softly, "though perhaps not quite like this." Suddenly, Rosie drew back, realizing that the painting told too much too explicitly about her and Juan. She was embarrassed. "This one is not for show. I wouldn't want anyone, especially not your mother to see it. I don't know what came over me. It sort of painted itself."

Rafaela stood back and considered the painting for a moment. "Yes, it is true. It may shock my mother. It may shock many people. But it will also move them. You must include it."

"No, I couldn't. I'll paint others that aren't so . . . so shocking. Please don't tell anyone about this."

"Rosa, I think you are wrong to hide it like you try to hide the love for my brother. Besides, it is not so recognizable as you and Juan. There are so many flowers and vines covering the lovers in the painting, almost like they were wearing clothes."

"I'll think about it."

As she washed her brushes and chatted with Rafaela, she suddenly noticed that Rafaela held an envelope in her hand. "It's from Juan," said Rafaela uneasily. "It just arrived; I came up here to tell you."

"Oh," Rosie felt her heart pound, but she tried to sound calm. "What did he have to say?"

"Would you like to read it?"

"It's in Spanish, I imagine . . ."

"I'll translate anything you don't understand."

Rosie's hands shook as she opened the envelope. It was addressed to his mother "and family." Rosie hoped that she would at least be mentioned by name in the letter. Even a postscript would be better than nothing. But it was a short, factual letter with press clipping reviews of his concerts enclosed. He also mentioned that he would be arriving home soon and looked forward to seeing them all. "All" became a precious word to Rosie; it had a general ring to it that did not specifically exclude her. As tiny a word as it was, it gave her a mountain of hope.

After a hearty lunch, she took a freshly stretched canvas and walked to the charming Plaza del Potro where the façades existed back in the time of Cervantes. At the top of an old fountain dating back to the sixteenth century was a horse rearing up. It was the plaza where the buggy drivers still brought their thirsty horses to drink.

She wanted to make one of these old-fashioned buggies the subject of one of her paintings and, as had happened with most of her paintings lately, the subject took on an unexpected, highly surrealistic turn. She superimposed the horse drawn carriage over the red tiled Cordovan rooftops that she was used to viewing from the top of the Conejo Blanco.

The horse was a charging white stallion and the buggy a glittering black with red wheels. In it she and Juan soared across a luminous blue Cordovan sky at dusk, the setting sun casting gold shadows on their translucent skin, Rosie's long blond hair flowed out behind them in the wind, making a long tail of stars, like a comet.

The flying sensation was what she had felt the night they had made love together, soaring like lightening across the soft Andalusian sky. He would be home soon. It was all she could think about. Her love would be home.

Chapter Thirteen

ROSIE HAD NOT heard from the bullfighter Manuel Herrera since the *feria* in Seville, though Danny once mentioned reading that he was in South America. She thought very little about him, except in a very general sense. Bullfighting had piqued her interest. She returned many times to the bullfight museum in Cordoba, wandering slowly through the exhibits. There were very few visitors so the guard, who was an *aficionado*, had time to explain much to her. He was an elderly man who had assisted Manolete in his youth, and he told many stories of the famous *torero*. She asked him once what he thought of Manuel Herrera and the man winced. "He is another follower of El Cordobés. Both could have been better than the best—but they play to the crowds. It is all for the money now, not for the love of the bulls." She admired Manuel's courage, but did not know enough to argue the artistic merits of his style.

Rosie made several sketches of the old man, finding his craggy, timeworn face fascinating. She finally convinced him to pose for a portrait in front of the tiny crumbling house where Manolete was born. She had thought out the canvas weeks before in her mind and the work went very fast, better than she anticipated. It lacked the usual splashes of bright color that now characterized her work, but it had majesty and the old man's sense of courage and pride at being included with a monument to the person he had admired most in the world. Rosie had decided to do the painting a little after dawn to get a soft golden light with blue shadows. Also, she knew that if she began painting in the middle of the afternoon, she would be deluged by tourists peaking over her shoulder, asking questions and that would put the old man ill at ease.

Within an hour and a half she was finished, sitting back from the work and putting in the final touches. The old man nodded slowly, then cocked his head to an angle. "Is my nose really that long?"

Rosie laughed. "My painting is not supposed to reproduce you exactly. You must have a photograph taken for that."

"But it is *very* good," he apologized. "I think, on the whole, you make me look better than I am!"

Suddenly she heard a car horn. There had been no automobiles in the tiny square that morning. She and the old man turned and saw a long black limousine pull up. A man jumped out and rushed up to them. "Rosa! I thought it was you!"

The old man gasped in astonishment. "It is Manuel Herrera."

"And what an extraordinary painting—in front of Manolete's house! You were a bullfighter once, *viejo*?" Manuel asked the man.

"No. But I assisted the best!" He nodded toward the house.

Rosie noted in Manuel an almost religious respect for the master, and it amused her to see a man so sure of himself show that he admired something. She wondered if he might be embarrassed at catering to the commercial side of his art.

"You are certainly up at the crack of dawn," Rosie commented. "I got up early to catch the light. What is your excuse?"

"I am just getting home from a party," he explained.

"But you say you are here catching light?" He looked strangely at her. "Can one *catch* light?" he laughed delightedly. "Can one *catch* sunbeams and moonbeams?"

"That is what artists are for," she responded. "I hide in the grey shadows and wait until they peak over the rooftops, then I grab them in my hands and quickly spread them all over my canvasses before they run away."

Manuel's eyes sparkled as she spoke. "Yes, I can see how you tricked the light onto your canvas. You have painted the elusive light of dawn on this man's face and infused him with the spirit of Manolete, for he also reflected the light of dawn."

The old man had been trying to understand the conversation but remained silent out of deference for Manuel Herrera and his celebrity status. But once he heard the name Manolete, he could no longer contain himself. "What are you saying?" he asked Manuel in Spanish.

"I have told this artist that she has miraculously given you the soul of Manolete."

He was pleased. "It is because I have told her much about the master. And she understands that, you see. This woman understands the *corrida*. It is not usual for an American, but she carries it in her soul."

A young woman leaned out of the limousine window. "Manuel, we are going to be late to meet the others for breakfast."

He walked back to the waiting car and gave instructions to the chauffeur. The car pulled away from the curb while Manuel returned to Rosie. The girl in the back seat leaned out of the window and shouted, "What's going on! What on earth are you doing?" He ignored her.

"That was not a very nice thing to do to your date," said Rosie.

"I only met her last night," he shrugged. "I told the chauffeur to take her to breakfast, and she will write home that she had breakfast with the chauffeur of Manuel Herrera. It is the next best thing, eh?"

"She won't think so."

"Pity," he said with indifference.

Rosie, for a moment, caught a glimpse of what it must be like to be a famous celebrity: a bullfighter, a rock star, a famous guitar virtuoso. With so many admirers, one more meant nothing. And he would never know if it was him or his fame that women wanted.

"I am surprised you remember me," she teased him, "with so many women running after you."

"I like you because you are an artist, with the heart and soul of one. Most of the women that men like Juan and I meet—they are rich with only air between their ears. They do not appreciate what we are and what we do. They like only the aspect of having their photographs in magazines and newspapers. But you, Rosa, you are one of us—an artist who awakes at dawn 'to catch the light.' It is no wonder my friend Juan fell madly in love with you. You are the kind of woman who inspires *conciertos*."

Rosie's heart pounded wildly at the mention of Juan. She was dying to ask Manuel more about him but was deathly afraid of what he might say. He might tell her that Juan was back with Jane Sidney in London, or perhaps he had taken up with another actress. She thought of the beautiful flamenco dancer who was once his mistress and Jane; both were artists in their own way. Juan did not run in circles of ordinary women. She was not a unique entity in his varied repertoire.

Manuel studied her painting closely. A genuine look of admiration crossed his face. "Juan told me you had a *corazón cordobés*. I think he was right. Even with your blond hair and green eyes. I saw it the morning you were dressed in Andalusian costume at the *feria* with your hair pulled back and the white rose."

They later sat at one of the sidewalk restaurants in the plaza and had a light breakfast of coffee and rolls. Suddenly Rosie grew serious, remembering with a rush the events of the last evening they were all together at the *feria*. "Manuel, why did you lie to Juan, telling him that we had been lovers?"

"Ay," he looked skyward with a sigh. "I am rarely afraid of the bulls, but of my friend Arévalo's hands, the precious talented hands that produce music like no one else in the world . . . that he would use them to . . . But then you must have heard everything in the hall, eh?"

"Yes," she admitted and then angrily, "I don't know why you had to tell him that we had made love."

"It was only meant to be a joke. Please do not be offended, Rosa, but we have had many jokes like that. I had no idea that he would be so upset."

"But you told him later, didn't you? That it was all a lie?"

Manuel considered a moment, squinting his eyes, trying to recall the evening. Finally he shook his head. "I don't remember, but I don't think so. I was going to tell him the next morning but by the time I awoke, he had left."

The chauffeur finally returned—without the young, disappointed woman from earlier. "Listen, Rosa, a Countess, a good friend of mine who lives up on the hill is throwing a party for me tonight. I would like to take you as my guest."

"The Countess! Yes, I know her. She has been very kind to me. She arranged for my paintings to be represented by Señora Calderón in Madrid."

"Calderón is handling your paintings?" his eyes widened. "Do you know her?"

"She is the most famous, the shrewdest art agent in Europe. Any artist of importance in the last twenty-five years owes his success to her. She takes only a very few, and those she chooses always do well. But she is very strict. It is because of a solid reputation she has built with gallery owners and dealers. They can always depend on her people to deliver. You must be careful never to disappoint her. I had a good friend, a talented sculptor. She made a lot of money and fame for him, but he began to drink and forgot to put his work in order. And now there is no one of any importance in Europe who will handle his work, because Calderón said he could not be trusted."

"But if he is talented, isn't that all that matters?"

"I may be the best bullfighter in Spain, but if I do not show up to several fights, how long do you think they will continue to book me in the major rings, eh?"

"I see what you mean," said Rosie thoughtfully.

"But what do you say to going to the Countess's party tonight?"

"I would love to, Manuel. In fact, the Countess has

invited me there before, but I've always had to say no! You see, the clothes I have with me: jeans, T-shirts, a few skirts and blouses. Nothing to wear to a Countess's party, not the way I understand she entertains."

"Ah, but you could come in jeans and everyone would applaud your originality! You forget we are Spaniards!"

"It wouldn't be right, Manuel, really—but I thank you for the invitation."

He took her hand and led her to the waiting limousine. "I will not accept your rejection so easily, especially on so slim an excuse as not having a dress to wear."

He gave the driver directions to a Madame Charlotte's. Rosie thought it sounded like a house of ill repute, but it was an elegant French boutique. Madame Charlotte made a great fuss over Manuel. "It will be no great problem to find a dress for her. With a figure like that and her coloring. She can wear anything!"

After trying on several dresses, they all finally settled on a midnight blue silk. It was very simple and décolleté. Madame Charlotte provided the accessories and jewelry to finish the high fashion look. All the time she was trying on dresses, Rosie caught glimpses of the price tags. There was nothing under $300, and she wondered just what sort of arrangement was being made to pay for the dress. "Manuel," she whispered. "All this is lovely, but it is *very* expensive. I don't have $300 and I certainly don't want you to pay for it."

"Don't worry," he assured her, but when she emerged from the dressing room, she saw Manuel handing Madame Charlotte's cashier a credit card.

"Manuel, I won't let you do this," she took him aside angrily. "It's so . . . so . . ."

"For me, it is no different if I buy you a rose or a dress. I can well afford it."

"That's not the point."

"You mustn't feel it compromises you, Rosa. It is a gift, freely given without strings."

"But to spend that much money on a *dress*. It insults my Kansas good sense."

Madame Charlotte came over to them. "I shall not be discreet for I overhear your conversation and I have a suggestion for you. There is a wealthy woman who buys her clothes here. She has a charity store where the women like her, who can only wear a dress once, can take their clothes. I will take your dress there after the party and it will go to a good cause."

"But it will never fetch the original price it did here," protested Rosie.

"Ah, but you are mistaken, mademoiselle. Do you not think a woman would pay very dear to wear the dress that Manuel Herrera's love wore? The legend makes the dress more valuable than my own price tag. There is not a woman in Europe who does not have a fantasy to be loved, even for only a night, by the dashing bullfighter, Manuel Herrera."

Rosie found it difficult to dispute the French logic. "Yes, I guess it's like all those quaint inns in America that claim 'George Washington slept here.'" She hadn't meant the double entendre, and when it came out she blushed scarlet, but they all laughed.

"How charming you are," pronounced Madame Charlotte. "It is no wonder Monsieur Herrera wants to make you expensive gifts."

Rosie was stunned at how quickly it was assumed she was his mistress. She did not like feeling owned by Manuel Herrera any more than she liked Juan's assuming she was his sole property. She was an artist in her own right, building a solid career. One day she might even be as famous as Manuel Herrera or Juan de Arévalo! It was a heady thought and gave her confidence.

When Manuel returned with her to the Conejo Blanco, he also extended the party invitation to Rafaela and Danny, but they declined. It was a Saturday night and the restaurant would be too packed to leave Señora Gómez alone.

The Señora was so excited about Rosie's date that she left the kitchen early to help her dress for the party. "What am I going to do about my hair?" Rosie asked her in genuine distress. She had washed and set it, but taken the rollers out too early and it hung lazily in droopy curls.

"You must wear it like you did the day of the *feria*, Rosa. I have never seen you look so beautiful as that day. I will fix it for you. It makes you look like a blond *cordobesa*. And you must wear a rose, just as you did that day. I will get one from one of the bushes in the patio."

When she had finished dressing with the midnight blue gown and her hair swept back with the rose, she did admit that it gave her a Spanish air. Danny whistled. "My little sister!" he laughed. "What a knockout!"

Manuel's mouth fell open when he saw her descend the stairs into the patio. Early guests to the restaurant also stopped eating and drinking to admire the beauty passing before them.

Rosie was surprised to encounter such a modern home in the midst of so much history, but the Countess had commissioned the unusual home from one of the students of Gaudí. It had more the look of the future than of the past. Rosie decided it belonged to Beverly Hills, California rather than to Cordoba, Spain. The swimming pool was constructed like a moat encircling the house, which rose up in the center island, resembling a modernistic concrete sculpture. Some of the guests were already in the pool, swimming, as far as Rosie could tell, stark naked. Despite the futuristic trappings, Rosie got the feeling she was watching an old Roman orgy. Remembering Cordoba's Roman past, she thought perhaps it was in keeping.

The atmosphere inside was more subdued. At least people were clothed, but Rosie had the distinct feeling that that might not last long. No wonder Manuel had attached so little importance to what she would wear. These were the beautiful people who had had too much money for too many centuries. It didn't matter what they did for thrills to break up the stultifying boredom of their meaningless, trivial lives. Rosie felt renewed respect for Juan de Arévalo who, in spite of his vast inherited wealth, had managed to do something constructive with his life.

Manuel Herrera knew quite a few of the people, and

from the cold stares she received from several young women, Rosie realized that she was confronting some of his ex-mistresses.

The Countess was surprised but delighted to see Rosie. "My dearest Rose, all those invitations of mine that you declined, and here I thought you were such a dedicated young artist. You only needed the divine splash and dash of a matador to rouse you out of your dear little shell. But I am so glad to see you. How ravishing you look in that dress. And you always claimed you had nothing to wear!"

"But I just got this," she stammered.

The Countess gave Manuel a sidelong glance. "You devil of a toreador, darling. You've been to Madame Charlotte's. Well, I couldn't be happier. It's time we introduced dear Rose to the public. She's going to captivate us all in time. Calderón is seeing to that, and how pleased she will be that *you* are escorting her around. But *I* discovered her. If it had not been for my keen eye, our dear Rose would have wasted away, her vast talents unrecognized, unrewarded. She would have flown back to Kansas on the wings of obscurity, and we would have all been the poorer for our loss."

With glib remarks, the Countess pretended to kiss Manuel delicately on the cheek, so as not to smudge her lipstick, and as Rosie watched her glide about the room, kissed her other guests the same detached way.

Manuel plucked a glass of champagne from the tray of a passing waiter and offered it to Rosie. She had never cared much for the bubbly liquid, but it was something to hold in her hand, and the entire scene was making her very ill at ease. If Manuel noticed her discomfort, he said nothing, happy to introduce her to his friends as an *American artist*. It might have made her proud that a famous bullfighter would give her a title of sorts, but it seemed only an excuse to justify her being there if she did not have a legitimate title like Countess or marquesa.

"Would you like to see the rest of the house?" he asked her. She nodded eagerly. Not that bizarre things interested her, but she was anxious to get away from the smoke-filled room they were in. Once upstairs, she noticed that some of the rooms contained guests in embarrassing situations—embarrassing to Rosie, that is. They did not seem to mind doors being opened on them. Rosie quickly suggested they return downstairs to join the others.

Just as they arrived at the bottom of the stairs, Rosie's heart stopped. Juan de Arévalo was standing in the hallway talking to the Countess. On his arm was Jane Sidney.

Chapter Fourteen

"WELL, LOOK WHO'S HERE!" bubbled Jane and hugged Manuel dramatically.

"That is what I was about to say," laughed Manuel. "All of us have not been together since the *feria* in Seville." Rosie had the odd sense of having heard these same words before. It was at the *feria* when other friends of Juan's and Manuel's said the same things. Did they all run in and out of each other's lives in a series of parties and *ferias*? "But then I was in South America, Juan was in London, Rosie was in Cordoba and Jane . . . where were you?"

"London, darling." Jane winked.

Rosie looked to Juan for his reaction. So that was the real reason he had never returned her calls; he had been too busy with Jane. He had not cared about her in the least! "You look well, Rosa," Juan said stiffly.

"Yes, what a lovely dress," enthused Jane. "You got it at Madame Charlotte's."

"Why, yes, how did you know?"

"I saw it there a few months ago—and then I happen to know that Manuel always goes there to buy dresses for his lady loves. But don't ask me how *I* know that," she laughed.

Juan now glared at Rosie. She wanted to explain that it was not an outright present, that it would go to charity after tonight, but she did not want to insult Manuel. Besides, it would be good for Juan to think another man would want to buy her expensive clothes. Perhaps he would even think she had been seeing Manuel. As long as he had been wrapped up with Jane Sidney, there was no reason for him to think she had been pining away alone in Cordoba.

"When did you get back to Cordoba?" she asked Juan.

"I just arrived tonight."

"And already at a party," mused Rosie sarcastically. "I suppose you will stop by the Conejo Blanco and give your regards to your family tomorrow."

"No, I was there tonight," he said slowly.

Rosie realized that he must have been there with Jane Sidney. She burned with rage that he would further want to humiliate her by flaunting his flashy mistress when he thought she would be there. It was underhanded and cruel beyond belief, the final insult! She was glad she had surprised him by being with Manuel Herrera at a Countess's party.

"A buffet dinner is being served in the dining room," announced the Countess. "Or if you would prefer, like me, you may go swimming in the pool."

"Oh, that sounds delightful on such a warm night," enthused Jane. "Come on Juan, let's go swimming."

"No, thanks. I haven't eaten yet."

Manuel turned to Rosie. "Would you like to swim?"

"No, thanks, you go ahead, if you wish."

Jane took his hand, "Oh, yes, Manuel! You come swimming with me. Juan is so stodgy about skinny dipping, in public, anyway. I *know* you're not, and it's been ages since I've seen all those charming little bullfighting scars on your handsome body."

"Don't worry about me," Rosie encouraged him.

"Well, all right, if Juan promises to look after you until I return."

"I don't need looking after; I'll do fine on my own," she answered.

Juan didn't answer, but nodded slightly at him. There was still no trace of a smile on his face. He had the look of a Velázquez painting, the tall, somber mystery of Andalusian nobility in his narrow face and dark eyes.

"Would you like to go to the buffet?" Juan asked her coldly when they were alone.

"I'm not very hungry, thank you." She looked away from him.

"I am." Turning away from her, he walked into the dining room. Rosie stood there for a minute staring at his back, then crossed the living room and stepped out on the balcony. She would not trot after him like a trained dog. If he wanted to talk to her, he could find her. She could take care of herself. Below in the pool, she could see Manuel and Jane frolicking together with the others, and it did not bother her. Amazed that she could be so indifferent to Manuel, she compared her reaction to the night of the *feria* with Juan when she had been so transported by jealousy.

The sight of Juan affected her in a more disturbing way than she imagined. Time had done nothing to dull the tumultuous feelings. But obviously, by the way he ignored her, the feelings had not been mutual. She wanted desperately to turn and see what he was doing inside; could he possibly even be watching her, or was he being sociable with another woman? If he were watching, she would not give him the satisfaction of knowing she was interested and kept her eyes glued to the panorama of the night sky.

Like the stars and galaxies splattered on a black canvas by white paint from a dry brush, she would paint herself in as a tiny blue insignificant dot at the corner. Insignificant among all the bright luminaries, slightly out of place.

"What are you thinking, Rosa?" she heard Juan's voice behind her. It was low, almost menacing.

For a second she considered spilling out all her tormented feelings, but opted instead for a description of the galaxy canvas she saw in the sky.

"But why would you make yourself such a small insignificant blue dot?" There was brief amusement in his voice.

"Yes, you're right, if I am painting a slice of the universe, I would not show up at all, not even as a dot."

"But it all depends on your perspective. You might paint the universe from this balcony and it would be partially framed by that willow tree. And when I was watching you from inside, I saw you very large in the frame. But that was *my* perspective."

"I'd rather consider it as an impersonal alien from outer space looking down here."

"You don't want to be involved?" he asked gently.

"Yes," she turned from him and walked away a few steps.

"Rosa, perhaps we should talk."

He was leaning against the rail, the night sky forming a dramatic backdrop for his chiseled features reflecting the chiaroscuro of light and shadow, the elusive *sol y sombra* of Spain. In that brief moment, she knew she'd never be free of him. If she never saw him again, that picture would lie indelibly etched on her brain. Every conscious moment, his dark eyes, looking at her just that way, would stare up at her from her own sketch pad, appear mysteriously in her paintings. Since that day in the Prado, he had never ceased to intrude on her every thought.

"If you are going to tell me that you and Jane Sidney are back together again and that you hope I'll understand, save your breath. We would be better off without words," she said bitterly.

"Would you believe me if I told you I haven't even seen Jane since the *feria* in Seville until this very night?"

"No."

"It's true."

"You didn't fly in from London with her?"

"I didn't even know she was *in* London, and even if I had, I would not have called her. We were rehearsing every-day and the concerts were exhausting."

"But you would have called her if you'd had the time, so it is a moot point. And how is it that you ended up here tonight with her on your arm? Mere coincidence?"

"Yes. She's a good friend of the Countess. I don't know how long she's been here. She saw me at the doorway, and we were just talking when you and Manuel came down the stairs."

"Oh, Juan," her voice was breaking with emotion, "How we do misunderstand each other!"

He began to move toward her, then reconsidered it. "But I see that you are very smitten with my friend Manuel. It did not take you long to forget me."

"That's not true! I just saw him this morning while I was

painting in front of Manolete's house. He asked me to this party and . . ." Juan was looking at her dress and she realized what he surmised. "Oh—you think because I let him buy me this dress—it's not like that at all." She explained how Madame Charlotte was going to take it to a charity where it would help raise money for the poor.

"Then you must take it to the charity yourself, if such a thing exists. I know Madame Charlotte. She will have it cleaned and hang it back on the rack at twice the original price, telling people that the exact same dress was purchased by Manuel Herrera for the woman he loves."

"But he doesn't love me. I'm simply his date for the night," she protested.

"His mistress for the night."

"Don't be absurd!" Her green eyes glinted with anger.

"If he takes you to a party at the Countess's, it is what he had in mind. You see what goes on below us in the swimming pool. You are not blind. Don't play the innocent. You were upstairs with him when I arrived."

Rosie gasped. "You have no right to insinuate anything from that! Odd as it may sound to your pruriant mind, he was just showing me the house!"

Juan walked slowly toward her and ran his hand down the rich midnight blue silk dress. "You might as well keep the dress," he said with disgust. "I'm sure you earned it. Was this the great love you were keeping yourself for, Rosie? The great passion with sincerity?" He pointed down to the swimming pool.

"I don't see where it should make a bit of difference to you, Juan," she hissed angrily, "I am not your property. When I tried to apologize to you, you did not even answer my phone calls. Not once did you ever bother to mention me, even as a postscript in a letter to your mother. I was willing to admit I was wrong, forget my pride. But you only wanted to hurt me. Well, congratulations. You have finally done it. Not even your silence all these months has hurt me as much as what you have just said. You may not believe that I have not been involved with Manuel, not the night of the *feria*, not ever, but it doesn't matter. You have absolutely no claims on me. I can go with Manuel or anyone else I want to, upstairs or in the pool. *You* were the one who set me free!"

"Rosa. . . ," he touched her shoulder, but she pulled away.

"Leave me alone. That's what you intended to do anyway. You told me that. I will leave Cordoba if you want to visit with your family. I will leave Spain. As long as I never have to see you again as long as I live!"

"Rosa, my Rosa," he pressed her to him as she sobbed. "You told me you despised me. I believed you! If I had only known you felt as I did. I have been crazy in love with you. I could have killed Manuel the night of the *feria* over love for you." He kissed the tears from her cheeks. "The last thing in the world I want is for you to leave Cordoba, or Spain—not without me, not ever again. I want you forever. That is why I went directly to the Conejo Blanco when I arrived tonight, hoping to talk to you there. When they told me you had come here, I had to find out for myself."

"Find out what?" she looked up at him confused.

"Oh, my Rosa, my beautiful, lovely Rosa," he hugged her tightly. "Don't you understand? I want to marry you. I want to live my entire life with you by my side."

"Marry me?" she said in a weak voice. "Oh, Juan," she buried her head against his shoulder. He lifted her face and kissed her passionately. They clung together tightly, letting all the sorrow of the past months drift like vapor out into the soft Cordovan night.

"You accept my proposal?" he held her at arm's length.

She threw her arms around his neck. "Of course I accept. I am the happiest woman in the world. You cannot know how much I love you, Juan!"

"Good," he laughed. "Then let's get out of this decadent awful place," he took her hand. "We'll go back to the Conejo Blanco and have my mother open a bottle of her finest sherry. Tonight we celebrate our engagement!"

She turned to look back out at the stars. "I shall make

this painting after all," she said softly. "And we shall both be very large on the canvas. I'll put that willow tree in and beyond, the whole universe opening up for us."

They drove swiftly down off the hill in Juan's red sports car, the wind blowing Rosie's blond hair out behind her. She thought of the painting she had done of the two of them in the Cordovan buggy, their winged chariot. He reached for her hand and held it to his lips. How much more thrilling it was actually being next to him than having to imagine him in paintings.

"I have so much to tell you, Juan. So many things have happened in my life. I've been painting every day since you left."

"I want to see your work, *mi amor*. I want to know everything about you."

As they reached the outskirts of Cordoba, crossing the old Roman bridge, Juan suddenly pulled over and stopped the car. "You know that it is still early." He slipped his arms around her and she fell willingly into his arms.

"Not here, Juan," she giggled as his lips moved sensuously down her long neck.

"Then what do you say we go to my house first, then back to my mother's for the announcement. Perhaps it is not the proper way to celebrate an engagement?"

"No, it is not proper at all," she said, looking seriously into his eyes.

He started the motor again and pulled back onto the road. "You're right, Rosa. We will go to my mother's now."

"But just because it isn't proper doesn't mean that we are bound by convention." She gave him a twinkling sidelong glance that held erotic promise.

"You are right, *mi amor*!" he threw back his head and laughed. His white teeth sparkled in the moonlight. "You and I are two free spirits in the night. We will never be bound by convention, not tonight, not any night! We are two artists and whatever we do will be right because we do it."

When he opened the door to the Arévalo *palacio*, he took her by the hand and led her quietly into the hallway.

"You will be the new Marquesa de Arévalo," he whispered. "*Mi vida, mi amor*—my life, my love."

She could see the huge, elegantly framed Francisco Goya painting, and it made her shudder to think that she would be sharing a home with so many awesome works of art.

"Juan, I'll try to make you happy," she said softly.

He was leading her to the thickly carpeted staircase winding up to the next floor. "Tonight, we shall make love as though it were the first time. An opening night gala concert. And each night we are married and make love we shall remember this night above all of them, and we will make it better. Each time will be better than the last."

He opened a carved oak door. There was a large Spanish bed and Mediterranean-style furniture of heavy, dark stained wood. "This will be *our* room now, Rosa "

"Oh, how I love you, Juan," she sighed as her midnight blue silk dress fell to the floor and Juan kissed her bare white shoulders.

Chapter Fifteen

ROSIE WAS SO burning with passion for Juan that she would have rushed their lovemaking to completion. But Juan was orchestrating each moment of their love as a composer would each stanza; each note was a chromatic scale with grace notes and cadenzas and fiery staccatos.

Where once she had seen her body as his guitar, she now realized that Juan used the entire symphony orchestra to express his love. When he kissed the tips of her breasts, she became a thousand sighing violins. She arched her back to receive his kisses, knowing that her body would rise and fall at his will. There were thundering drums, the primitive percussions pulsing through the lower half of her body. He was using his lips on her naked skin as a conductor used a baton, his long sensitive fingers making her sing with the whistling agony of a gypsy rhapsody.

"I know your very soul, my Rosa. I will make your soul sing with a passion you have never known."

She was pushing his head away. "It's too much, Juan . . . I've never . . . I cannot bear so much."

"Then you must have more," she felt his insistence grow stronger. "You must have so much that you burst with it," he whispered. He would not allow her to make him stop.

"No, Juan, please," she cried. "It is too much!"

"You're afraid of the depth of your own passion. Trust me, Rosa. Let it overcome you. You must let our passion be your master. It is only then that you will be free."

Mutely she obeyed him, relaxing, letting the sensations flow over and under, lifting her from their bed of love like a blossoming flower, opening its velvety petals one by one as she stretched the tendrils of her arms and legs around him in an ever tightening vinelike embrace.

"Ah, now you are beginning to understand, eh, Rosa?" he said hoarsely as he felt her tremble in his arms. "But it is only the beginning for you. Again, now again. Yes, Rosa, I want you to know my love, how deeply I love you, how I want to make you happy. Yes, Rosa, hold me tighter. Pull me into your soul, *mi amor. Eres mi alma, mi vida.* I shall become your soul."

"You are, you always have been my soul," she thought wildly. "I have always known you, Juan, even as a child. You were the Spain I longed for without knowing why. You are what was always missing from my life, my reason to live and create."

"You are tired, *mi querida?*" He pushed the strands of long blond hair from her small face and kissed her damp forehead. "We shall rest for a moment, then begin again, eh?"

She brushed the warm hollows of his neck with her lips. "Juan, oh, Juan," she whispered breathlessly. He pulled her tighter against him. "I thought that night in Seville was beyond anything I had ever imagined with a man—but this . . . this is . . ."

"What?" she could feel him smile as the tips of her fingers crossed over his lips.

"I don't have words, Juan. I must do a painting for you. All my paintings are for you, about you. It's all I've thought about since you left."

"So you have done paintings of *me?*" There was a hint of flattered ego in his deep, resonant voice.

"Well, only one you might recognize—but they are all you in one way or another—guitars and flowers. I tried to paint the way your music made me feel, the way *you* made me feel. But in my sketchbooks, and I haven't shown them to anyone, I have let my fantasies go wild."

"You must show them to me," he ran his hand down her back and she shuddered again under his touch.

"I don't know if I should, Juan. I'd be embarrassed to show you; they're so flagrantly erotic."

"But you are not embarrassed to make passionate love to me. Why can't you show me your drawings?"

"You might laugh at them."

"*Mi amor*, I would never laugh at them. They are part of you and I love you! You must never keep any secrets from me, not even your sketchbooks. You must share everything with me and I shall share all my music with you. You will hear all the mistakes I make when I am learning a new piece. You will hear me swear and say terrible things to my guitar, you will hear me struggle with the piano whose keys always conspire to elude me. What is unique about our love, Rosa, is that we are artists; we can accept the trials and errors of each other's work. We can bolster each other up and give encouragement when it's needed. And we can also offer good criticism when that is needed. Your paintings will inspire me, and my music shall do the same for you."

They could not stop smiling as they walked into the Conejo Blanco together after midnight. Rosie was sure, from the glow she felt radiating from her, that everyone must know that they had just made love for hours.

Señora Gómez was sitting at a table with some old friends. A smile lit up her face when she saw Rosie and Juan walk in arm in arm, so obviously in love.

Juan kissed his mother tenderly on the cheek and said, "I did exactly as you wished. I went to the Countess's and spirited Rosie away. And now we want you to be the first to know that we are engaged to be married."

"Señora Gómez put her hand to her mouth and then placed it on her heart. Tears brimmed in her large dark eyes. She rose quickly from her chair and hugged them both. "I have not been so happy since Rafaela and Danny told me they were getting married. How lucky a woman I am to have a daughter-in-law and a son-in-law who I love like my own children!"

As soon as Danny and Rafaela heard the news, they brought out the good sherry to celebrate. The Conejo Blanco closed its doors to the public, but whoever was already there joined in the celebration. Juan played the guitar and they all danced. Even the Señora danced with Juan, looking younger than her years, girlishly delirious with joy.

Rosie was drunk with her own happiness. Each time she looked at Juan, she thought of the hours they had just spent together, and his penetrating dark eyes told her that he also shared the thought. Nothing could ever go wrong in her life again. She had the man she loved and a future career based on the art she loved.

"When is the date?" Rafaela asked them. The guests had all gone home and just the family remained, drinking strong espresso coffee in tiny demitasses.

"We'll get married immediately, maybe tomorrow," laughed Juan, leaning over to give Rosie a kiss.

"But that's so soon," said Señora Gómez practically. "There is so much to do. Rosie's dress, the invitations to our friends."

"Oh no, please don't go to any trouble. Just the immediate family," begged Rosie. "I've never wanted a big wedding. Juan, you don't want a lot of people, do you?"

"Well, perhaps we can have a party when we get back from Paris, but I agree—only the family at the wedding."

"You're going to Paris?" asked Danny.

Rosie looked at Juan with surprise. "What's this about Paris?"

"I have several concerts scheduled there next week. That's why I wanted to get married right away. We can go there for the concerts, then afterwards we can honeymoon through the chateau country. There is a beautiful chateau just outside of Tours, Chateau d'Artigny, that has been converted into a luxury hotel. You can do paintings of the Loire Valley."

"But, Rosie, what about your gallery opening in Madrid?" Danny reminded her. "You have only four weeks and another ten paintings to do?"

"Gallery opening?" asked Juan with surprise.

"Yes, my darling, I didn't have a chance to tell you, but the Countess put me in touch with an agent in Madrid, Señora Calderón, and she is arranging a show for me! It's all very exciting. From what I understand, Calderón is one of the best agents in Europe."

"That she is," he said thoughtfully. "I had no idea. Rosie, this is wonderful for you."

"Her work is so beautiful, Juan, you must see it," said Rafaela enthusiastically. "I told her it is like the way you play the guitar. It goes directly to your heart. What a wonderful marriage you both will have, Rosie with her paintings and you with your music."

"Come, would you like to see the paintings now?" Rosie asked him eagerly.

"Oh no, *mi amor*, not tonight. I am too tired, and I want to see them all when I am fresh and can appreciate them."

Rosie was not sure what had changed between them, but she sensed that Juan was not altogether happy about her success. Was he jealous? Did he think that her career took away from his?"

She had never thought Juan to be a man who would want a woman to subjugate her career for his, he had seemed so supportive about her work—and yet there was an undefinable look in the depths of his dark eyes that had not been there before.

"But, Rosa," said the Señora brightly, "You must simply call this Señora Calderón and tell her to postpone your gallery opening. She will understand that you are getting married and that love takes precedence in this case!"

Rosie remembered what Señora Calderón had said. The words echoed menacingly on her brain, "Women will produce a great number of paintings, then they are seduced by the old myths of love and marriage. They begin to defer everything to their husbands, and all their creative genius is repressed. A few have been able to continue with great works, but most begin to forget about deadlines and obligations. I will not tolerate that." Even Manuel Herrera had said that Calderón would drop her if she missed a gallery opening. And if she did, nobody would want to handle her work.

"Yes, *mi vida*," said Juan. "We must call Señora Calderón in the morning and tell her to make your opening another time."

"But I can't do that, Juan. If I do, she will drop me as a client."

"That's ridiculous. Why would she do that?" Rosie could see a hint of anger in his eyes, the muscles of his narrow face tense.

"Because she told me she would. She places a lot of importance on her artists making deadlines."

"But this is a problem that is quite simply solved," said Rafaela. "Rosie can take her paints and canvasses to Paris and work while she is there."

"She should not work on her honeymoon," Juan said sternly.

"But you will be doing concerts; what is the difference?" Rosie felt her cheeks grow hot.

Juan suddenly smiled. "You are right. You must take your paints and work there."

"I don't know," Rosie said softly. "All my work has been centered around Cordoba. It's the unifying theme of the exhibit. It is what Calderón liked. If I go to Paris ... the light is different, the surroundings. To cart my equipment in and out of a hotel—I must paint outside and I don't know the city. It would take weeks just to get oriented. And I'm all set up here to work. Juan, why can't we get married now? You can go to Paris, and I will stay here and finish my work. Then after my opening we can take our honeymoon. There is no reason we have to follow convention. Weren't you the one who said that? We have a whole lifetime to be together. A few weeks now at the beginning won't make that much difference."

"A wife should travel with her husband. It is not right that we should be apart," he said, his anger resuming. "It's a matter of principle."

"It is true," agreed Señora Gómez. "Your husband must come first, Rosa."

"I will give up my exhibit only on the condition that Juan gives up his concert in Paris," she said stiffly.

"But I am committed to those concerts. They have been booked long in advance."

"And so has my exhibit."

They stared angrily at each other. All the previous joy of the evening had vanished. They were at an impasse.

"If we are to be married, then we are together," he said strongly, his eyes flashing.

"If we are to be married, then we are together equally. I will not accept being less important than you, Juan. You must respect what I do."

"We're all tired," said Danny, placatingly. "Let's talk about this in the morning."

"Yes, in the morning, we will all see things with clear eyes," agreed Señora Gómez nervously. Rosie heard her say quietly to Juan in Spanish, "I will talk to Rosa for you. Don't worry, I will make her see that to marry a Spaniard, a woman must sacrifice certain things."

More than anything that had been said, this infuriated Rosie. She had worked too long and hard at her art to see it all dashed to the wind just at the moment she was becoming a success. Perhaps the Spaniards didn't understand that a woman needed the pride of accomplishment just as much as a man. But she would not let it go, not even if it meant the ultimate sacrifice of the only man she had ever really loved.

Juan leaned over and kissed her at the iron gate. The others had gone back into the restaurant, and they stood alone in the entry way, inhaling the fragrance of jasmine from the Señora's potted plants that lined the whitewashed wall.

Once she felt his body pressed so tightly up against hers, she forgot that there had been any dissension between them. Perhaps she was wrong. This wondrous feeling of being loved so passionately was worth everything else in the world.

Their lips parted and he searched for her. "Oh, Juan," she gasped, "I love you so much."

"We are meant to be together forever, *mi amor*," he reached down her silk dress and caressed her breasts. The

surging rhapsodies once again filled her. "How wonderful
it will be to sleep together every night in our own bed."

She thought of the high Spanish bed and the intoxicating
hours they had trembled in each other's arms. She longed
to have him again that night, to cradle her head in the
comfortable hollow between his shoulder and his strong
neck and sleep as she had at his ranch.

"You feel as I do, Rosa. Tomorrow we will talk again.
I know you will agree with me."

"I love you, Juan," she said, preferring not to argue
again. As she turned away from him and locked the heavy
gate behind her, she knew that her decision had already
been made.

Chapter Sixteen

ROSIE FOUND IT impossible to sleep that night. She tossed and turned, half the time wishing that Juan's lean muscular body was wound around hers, his strong hands calming her frazzled nerves. How could she possibly tell him that she could not marry him. He would not understand. Perhaps when he saw her paintings he would know. But he would also see how important he was to her. Perhaps then he would agree to letting her stay in Cordoba to work on the exhibit. Compromise. It only needed compromise. It was so simple, she thought wildly. But somehow she knew deep in her soul, that Juan de Arévalo would never agree to a marriage that was not on his terms.

Towards dawn, she slipped out of bed and went up to the roof. It was the time of day she loved most in Cordoba when the streets were quiet and illuminated by the pale blue light. It was a crucial time—just before the first rays of sunlight streaked over the olive covered hills and washed the white walls of the callejas golden and turned the brown walls of the Great Mosque and Alcazar a bright orange. It was just before the birds awoke and scurried from branch to branch in the trees, screeching at the lazy Cordovans to awaken.

She saw her life as quiet wisps of blue light reaching tentatively out toward day. When the bursting sun appeared, she wanted to grab hold of its fiery body and clutch it to her, embrace all its burning glory, consume it whole and let it make her glow scarlet white from within.

But when the sun did appear over the Andalusian hills,

Rosie found she could not look at its face, for it blinded her and made her turn away.

She saw Señora Gómez coming up the stairs toward her. "I like the roof at dawn, too," she told Rosie softly. "My life is so filled with people day and night and that makes me happy, but sometimes a woman needs these few minutes alone, this breath of pure air in your lungs. When you are married with little children, you will feel this way, too, Rosa."

Rosie ran her hand nervously through her long blond hair. She must tell the *Señora*. "I cannot marry Juan if he does not understand about my art," she said haltingly.

The older woman looked confused and sat down next to Rosie, putting her arm around her shoulders. "But, Rosie, the most important thing in life is love. It is the only thing in life worth living for. To share life with the man you love, to bear his children. Do not make the same mistake I did. I sacrificed my love to pride. I would not take the Marqués de Arévalo on his terms because he could not marry me. And all my life I have had my pride, and finally I have the love of both of my children, but I was hollow and empty in a certain place inside my heart that, no matter how happy your life may be, is forever hollow. Only the man you love can fill it, make it complete."

Rosie took the Señora's hand and pressed it fondly. "I know what you are trying to tell me, but to use your same image—marrying Juan would fill that one place in my heart, but then the others would be empty, and my art is what has made my life worth living for too many years."

"But to get married does not mean giving up your art. Juan will fix you a studio in the Arévalo *palacio*. You will have servants to help you take care of your children. You will not need to paint for money. You can paint for the pure pleasure it gives you. How many artists have that advantage?"

Rosie thought again of Señora Calderón's warning words. "But I want to be more than just a Sunday artist. I know I am capable of more. Señora Calderón assured me.

An artist cannot create in a vacuum; an artist needs to be recognized and appreciated. What I want to communicate on my canvasses, I want the world to feel and know."

The Señora looked at her with large sad eyes. "That is all very true. But I have seen your canvasses and I know what inspires them. It is your love for Juan. If you lose him, perhaps you will go on for awhile, inspired by the anguish and pain of the lost love. Then what? Will you be a dried up old woman like Señora Calderón who thinks only of her business? What will your paintings communicate to the world then?"

Everyone in the family seemed to have an opinion about her dilemma. Danny spoke to her after breakfast as she sat in the sunshine in the patio, drying her hair. "I know how important your art is to you," he began. "And if your reasons for not marrying Juan are only because you feel he will interfere with your career, then I will back you up, Rosie. But I think it's over a lot of rhetoric you have digested, and it doesn't begin to touch on the real reason you are backing away."

"Rosie brushed her long blond hair vigorously and glared at her brother. "What do you mean by that?"

"Is it your art or is it Chip?"

"I have forgotten all about Chip!" she snapped.

"Don't get so fired up."

"I'm not fired up," she threw her head back and narrowed her eyes. "Chip doesn't mean a thing to me anymore. I never realized how shallow a relationship we had before. If I had stayed in Wichita and married him, I would never have been able to accomplish what I have with my art. The best thing he could have done for me is to leave."

"Your hands are shaking, Rosie."

"That's because I'm nervous about Juan and what I'm going to say to him when he arrives in a few minutes. It won't be easy to tell him."

"Then you better tell him the truth," said Danny flatly.

"The truth is that my art, my career comes first."

"The truth is, dear sister, that you are afraid he will leave you like Chip did. You want to turn him away before he has the chance to hurt you. I had hoped that Juan de Arévalo, if nothing else, would open you up again to love, but you are determined to close yourself off from it. You're so afraid and panicked that you hide behind easy banners titled 'art' and 'career.'"

"Danny, that's not true at all!" she nearly yelled at him, and choked back her tears. How true it was, she really wasn't sure, but he had touched a sensitive chord. She had been hurt by Chip more deeply than she suspected and, though she did worry about Señora Calderón and her gallery opening, she knew that what her brother said had a ring of truth. Blaming it on her art *was* an easy out.

She was still distraught and unable to think clearly when Juan walked through the gate. He was in his faded denims with a cotton rust-colored shirt, the sleeves rolled partially up. She could see his tan lean chest where she had lain her head the night before, the strong arms that had held her in a dizzying embrace. The thin denims clung seductively to his well muscled thighs and she remembered, too, how they had felt pressed against her.

He stared down at her for a moment, his dark eyes crossing over her in the way that made her tremble. "Your golden hair reflects the sunlight." He took a strand of it, then gathered it all up in his hand and pulled her head back for a kiss. Her lips parted and she tasted the delicious warm scent of him wrapping around her. She reached her slender arms around his strong neck, touching the thick black hair. "Did you sleep well, Rosa?" he smiled.

"No, not very well," she admitted.

"I did not either. We will never sleep well again until we spend every night in each other's arms."

She saw the family coming toward them. Another emotional family confrontation was to be avoided. They had confused her with all their theories. She and Juan must resolve their problems together, just the two of them. "Please, darling, let's go for a walk; let's go visit the Alcazar gardens. It's so green and peaceful there with the fountains and the flowers. We need to be alone to talk."

"We can go to my house to be alone."

"But I cannot think clearly there," she said. "Please, let's go to the gardens. If we go to your house, we ... we'll only ..."

"Yes?"

"Oh Juan!"

He grabbed her narrow waist and held her close, "Come, we'll go to my house, *our* house soon."

She was helpless when he held her like that. Every muscle, every nerve in her slender body cried out for him, yearned to be united with him.

As soon as they stepped inside his door, they clung together, covering each other's faces with tender kisses that grew more intense by the second. His strong hands moved down her back, then up again. "Rosa, let us make love first, then we'll talk. We will die if we do not have each other this very moment."

"But we *must* talk," she said weakly, allowing him to lead her up the winding staircase. She felt as though she would die without an outlet for her love.

But when he opened the door to his room, she felt him tense. She looked over to the bed and gasped.

Jane Sidney had the covers pulled up just over her large breasts, her flowing red hair spread out on a pillow, her milk white skin as silky as the satin sheets. "You brought *her*, have you, darling? Well, send the dear home and we'll have some fun, just the two of us."

Chapter Seventeen

ROSIE'S MOUTH FELL OPEN, but she could not speak.

"What are you doing here?" Juan asked angrily.

"What I usually do here," Jane shrugged. "Don't act like this is the first time you have ever returned home to find me in your bed. It's not like your servants allow in complete strangers. In fact, they seemed rather glad to see me again. So did you last night."

Rosie felt faint, then regaining her strength, broke away from Juan's vicelike grip and ran down the stairs.

"Rosa, wait! I did not know she was there." He caught up with her in the hall, before she could fly out the door. He led her into his private study with the bullfight paintings and gave her a glass of sherry.

"Juan . . . that woman . . . in our bed . . . She was here last night, after you left me?"

"Of course not! I saw her only those few moments at the Countess's. We were once lovers, Rosa, you knew that. I shall talk to her. She will understand that it is over." He tried to hug her to him, but she pulled away, and sat across the room from him on the piano bench. Absently, she ran her fingers across the smooth black and white ivory keys. The image of the flaming-haired actress lying so sensuously on the very spot where she and Juan had made love the night before had badly shaken her.

Clearly Juan ran with a fast crowd where a woman could walk into a man's house uninvited and wait for him in his bed. But why had Jane Sidney been so sure of finding him alone?

"What did you say to Jane last night to make her think that you wanted her?" Rosie asked suddenly.

He shrugged and stared thoughtfully out into the adjoining patio. "It was when I first walked in. I only said I was happy to see her. I was being polite."

"It must have been more," insisted Rosie.

"It is nothing, Rosa. Let's not even talk about it. It was an ugly scene upstairs just then. It will never happen again."

"But you must have said something to her. I cannot believe that a woman would do what she did without some encouragement."

"Juan, darling, why don't you tell your little friend what you said to me at the door?" Rosie wheeled around and saw Jane Sidney coming toward them. She was dressed now in a shimmering pink silk pantsuit that clashed flamboyantly with her hair. Her large breasts jiggled as she walked toward the bar and poured herself a glass of wine. "Well, go on Juan. Why don't you tell her?"

"I don't remember what I said," Juan glared at her.

Jane crossed the room casually with the glass in her hand and stood close to Juan, looking up into his eyes. Rosie felt her skin grow hot with jealous rage.

"You said I looked so sumptuous you could take a bite out of me, Juan."

"You're lying," he said, his eyes narrowing.

"You're always so attractive when you're angry, my dear marqués. But it is true," she turned to Rosie. "He just won't admit it."

"It's a lie, Rosa, don't listen to her."

"So protective you are of your new mistress," laughed Jane in a high-pitched theatrical manner. "But that's the way you always are at first. Has he asked you to be the new Marquesa de Arévalo yet, my dear? Don't worry, he will. That's the next step."

Rosie's eyes widened, but she still could not say anything.

Jane was the consummate actress and, sensing that she commanded the center stage, was not about to relinquish it, even when Juan told her angrily to leave.

"I haven't finished my wine yet, darling. And it's not like you dashing Cordovans to be so impolite." She seated herself on a dark leather chair and crossed her legs. "Well, my dear, you can look forward to his asking you to be the Marquesa de Arévalo, such a pretty title—and an adorable *palacio*, don't you think. Just a sweet little cottage to call home. But this is nothing. You will be sent into raptures by the villa on Capri. It's pink with white shutters, and there are purple plum trees in the yard. You're an artist? You'll love painting that. But only special mistresses get invited to the villa, the ones he is going to make marquesas."

"I want you out of here," Juan said blackly.

Jane took another sip of wine and gazed up at his glowering face through thickly mascaraed eyelashes, then turned back to Rosie. "Have you had the big fight yet, then? The one that puts an end to the marriage? Granted it will be a silly one, my dear, when you look back on it, but it will be effective. Perhaps it will be that *your* career gets in the way of *his* idea of marital bliss. Then poof! go all the lovely little fantasies and poof! Juan goes back to his only true love—his guitar. Isn't that right, Juan?"

Rosie could not bear to hear anymore. She ran through the house, the tears falling down her face. She could vaguely hear Jane Sidney's shrill laughter and Juan calling after her.

Once out onto the street, she knew the small *callejas* well enough now and quickly eluded Juan, zigzagging through the back alleys until she reached the stark white square of the Cristo de los Faroles. There she leaned against the iron railing that surrounded the simple iron cross and cried.

Chapter Eighteen

WHEN SHE FINALLY reached the Conejo Blanco, her family was in an uproar. "Juan was here until just a few minutes ago," said Rafaela. "He was very upset and wants you to call him the moment you arrive."

"Did he tell you what happened?" she asked weakly.

"No. He would not say—just that there had been a terrible misunderstanding. Rosa, you must call him right away. Here, he wrote down his phone number on a piece of paper in case you didn't have it."

Rosie took the paper, crumpled it up in her hand and threw it in the trash. Trudging upstairs, she changed into jeans and a T-shirt, the clothes she used for work, and packed a small canvas off to the Alcazar gardens, hoping the tranquility of the lush green surroundings would rub off on her.

There was a secluded place she liked just below the stairs. A small stone bench was embedded in an archway and partially covered over with hanging bougainvillaea vines. In the clearing was an exquisite fountain, and the sound of falling water had a calming effect on her. She had often come to this shady refuge in the heat of the midday, imagining that the hidden spot was a place lovers from the fifteenth century used to rendezvous. Perhaps it was here that the rugged red-haired Columbus and the beautiful dark-eyed Beatriz de Bobadilla met and spoke of love in hushed voices.

Today, she tried not to think of its romantic aspects, only its tranquil seclusion. Tourists rarely came here, for it was off the main pathway, and she could take advantage of the solitude to sort through her stormy thoughts.

What Jane Sidney said had hit too close to home. In her obnoxious way, Jane had even zeroed in on the very source of their argument—her career. Was this a pattern of Juan de Arévalo's? Did he court women, dangling the carrot of the marquisate before their eyes, then pull the magic carpet out from under their feet when it came too close? Perhaps he had inherited his father's aversion to marriage.

She remembered again how they had lain together in his high Spanish bed, the words of love that he had whispered. Could any man make love to a woman with such passion and not really be in love?

Rosie sighed. Juan de Arévalo was certainly capable of it. He was a performer, wasn't he? A man who could sit on a stage night after night and perform concerts could give a convincing performance in bed. Hadn't he once said he was a genius at making love? If it took telling a woman he loved her and wanted to marry her to make her sing just the way he wanted, he would not hesitate to do it.

No wonder Jane Sidney was so bitter, goaded into confronting him the way she did. Juan de Arévalo must have wounded her terribly. He must have promised her all those things, then shunted her aside without a thought, once he had squeezed all the passion from her.

But why, when there were so many women available to Juan, would he want to bind them so thoroughly to him? It must be the ego, Rosie concluded. He would not be content to have only a woman's body, just as he would not be content to play only mediocre guitar. His conquest of a woman's soul would be as important to him as the mastery of a *concierto*.

Rosie stared at the blank canvas. She had not been able to put down a single brush stroke. It would be as useless to work today as it was yesterday. How simple it had been, even in all her anguish, to create. All her pent-up energy had been poured into her work.

But now that energy was being absorbed by the very real

presence of the man she loved. Maybe Calderón was right, after all. A woman gave too much of herself to love. If she married Juan, she would always be doing something for him and her work would suffer. Was it better for her art to be in anguish over him than to actually have him?

But it wasn't Calderón, she knew, who had been proved right. It was Danny. Her brother had seen through her ruse. The ultimate terror was that Juan would leave her like Chip had done. She had realized that the moment she had seen Jane Sidney lying there in Juan's bed. Jane's cruel words had only reinforced the fear that Juan would leave her. That emotion far outweighed the joy she had felt when he told her he wanted to marry her. It was a fear that clutched at her throat whenever she thought of marrying Juan. Any man she came to love would present the same threat, and she would find a way to stop him short of marriage. At all costs, she would never let herself feel the shame and humiliation of being left just before a wedding. Not even Juan, had everything gone right, could have changed that.

She buried her face in her hands, resting her elbows on her knees, and listened to the quiet trickling of the fountain.

"Rosa, thank God I've found you!"

She looked up and saw Juan standing before her. He was removing her canvas and paints from the bench and sitting down next to her. "I thought you must be here from what you said this morning. But I have been all through the gardens looking for you, then I remembered this spot. Of course, it is where an artist would go."

All her former rage and anger from the morning's scene with Jane Sidney came back to her. "Leave me alone. Isn't there someone waiting in your bed?"

"That was a cruel, stupid thing to say, Rosa!" he all but growled. She saw the muscles grow tense around his mouth. "You ran off before I could explain."

"What is there to explain? Jane Sidney made it very clear."

"Jane Sidney was lying through her teeth. I don't know why she said those things. There was no truth in it, none at all. I never asked her to marry me."

"But what a *coincidence*, her mentioning the little fight about our careers."

"I don't know where she got that. Perhaps because we used to joke about our affair, that it was impossible to see each other very much because our schedules were so diverse and she used to kid me about being a marqués."

"What about Capri?"

"I took her to Capri a few times. I go every summer. She has gone there with others."

Rosie looked into his dark eyes, trying to discern from their unfathomable depths whether or not he was lying. It was impossible to tell. "I cannot believe that a woman would do what she did this morning without having been so bitterly disappointed and hurt that she would lash out cruelly."

"She is an actress. It was a show, Rosa. She was treating us like an audience. That woman plays so many different roles on stage and the screen that she cannot tell the difference between fantasy and real life. She probably did not even realize that she was hurting you. To her it was all an amusing play."

"I don't care much for your friend's idea of a joke," Rosie said flatly.

He reached out and touched her cheek, but she pushed his hand away. "Rosa, I'm sorry she did that. If I could start the day all over again I would have come with you here and we could have talked, just as you said. Please, *mi querida*, let us pretend that the horrible scene never happened and that it is still morning and we have just come here to talk. Do you know that lovers in the fifteenth century used to come to this very spot where you are sitting?"

Rosie's anger was melting away. Sitting so close to Juan, she was being drawn in by the magic she always felt in his presence. He realized that she was softening and he took her hand, pressing the tips of her fingers to his lips. *"Te quiero, mi amor,"* he said in a low voice.

"Juan . . . I . . ."

"Don't say another word. Just kiss me."

The surging fire passed through their lips and inflamed

their bodies. He moved closer and his strongly muscled thigh pressed up against hers.

She wished that they were not in so public a place, for she would have loved to strip off all their confining clothes and make love there under the dripping red bougainvillaea and climbing vines. It was as though all the lovers who had met there in the past centuries were whispering encouragement through the rushing waters of the fountain.

"Now, *mi amor*. We are back to normal. You wanted to come here to talk. So we shall talk."

She had forgotten for the moment what it was she had so desperately wanted to tell him. The morning seemed so long ago. And now that she and Juan were together again, their magnetic bodies touching, she could think of nothing beside her need to be near him.

"It was about what we said last night," she began. "About our wedding."

"Tomorrow. How about if we get married tomorrow? I can't wait much longer because I must be in Paris no later than Monday to begin rehearsals with the orchestra of the French national television. Two of the concerts are to be televised live."

She closed her eyes for a brief moment, then opened them again, focusing as clearly as she could on the dark luminosity of his compelling eyes. "Juan, I must complete the paintings for my exhibit. It's very important to me. You must understand that."

"You can postpone the exhibit. I thought we had decided that. Isn't our marriage more important than your exhibit?" He was beginning to be angry again. "Rosa, you are talking foolishly."

"Am I?"

"Yes!"

"But you will not postpone your concerts in Paris to take me on a honeymoon."

"They are two different things!"

"They are the same!"

Juan stood up, his narrow dark face glowering with rage.

"You cannot love me as you say you do and want to stay here while I am alone in Paris."

"You cannot love me as you say you do and not want me to finish my paintings for the exhibit," she stood up and faced him squarely. This was not at all the fear of losing him. It was strictly a matter of principle. "We must be equal in a marriage."

"We *will* be equal. But this is ridiculous. It is nonsense to even argue about it!"

"If we cannot resolve this now, then there is no sense in even trying to make a marriage, Juan." She gathered up her canvas and paints, but he grabbed the canvas away from her.

"For this—for this empty canvas we are going to throw away a lifetime?" He tossed the canvas aside, and it fell into a flower bed.

The gesture was the final blow for Rosie. "Yes, I can see how you feel about my work."

"I didn't mean that, Rosa," he came after her trying to apologize.

She suddenly thought of Jane Sidney's pale face and the cruel mascaraed eyes. "What did you do to Jane—tear up a script in her face?" She spinned around to face him.

They stood glaring at each other, the quiet, lush gardens behind them. Rosie was suddenly reminded that the Alcazar had ceased to be a palace for monarchs in the sixteenth century and became the hideous headquarters of the Spanish Inquisition.

"It is you who have written this script, Rosa. And you can damn well write your own ending to it," he said with disgust and turned on his heel.

She watched him walk up the stairs toward the brown weathered buildings that had seen so much human suffering.

Once she and Juan had stood at the top of the tower and kissed. How arrogantly he sped up the stairs; how quickly he had taken the cue to walk out of her life.

She took a deep breath and realized she was clutching the empty canvas to her. For the first time in two days, she felt the deep, all-consuming urge to paint.

She hurried back to the secluded archway and set up her easel. The brush strokes came fast now and soon covered the canvas. She could not stop the haunting image of Juan's face, the angry scowl, his mouth set in a hard, unyielding line. She did not want to finish the canvas so quickly, for she knew that the moment she stopped, she would no longer be able to hold back the harsh tears that were threatening to explode inside her soul and send the fractured fragments scattering through the glowing fragrant flowers of the Alcazar garden.

Chapter Nineteen

"JUAN IS HERE to say goodbye. He leaves for Paris this afternoon. Won't you come downstairs, Rosa?" Rafaela pleaded with her, but to no avail.

"I'll be recovered by the time he gets back, or perhaps I'll take a trip then so I won't cause the family any discomfort. He's your brother, Rafaela, and I feel terrible about being so impolite, but to see him again right now— I just couldn't."

"It is not for me or my mother, Rosa, but for *you*. I know very well that you love him and that he loves you. If you could just talk it over . . ."

"Talking is what got us into trouble in the first place. If we didn't have to talk, everything would be fine."

Rafaela shook her head and left Rosie on the roof with her paintings. She had been painting furiously since the day in the Alcazar. If anything, her paintings were more violently emotional than before. She looked at the softly lyrical canvasses she had done even a week ago, the lovers under a tree, flying across the sky. Her colors were darker now, more intense. There were the midnight blues of her silk dress, of the Cordovan sky and the flaming scarlet of Jane Sidney's hair sweeping out like a malevolent comet seeking to destroy the earth.

Just as Marcel Duchamp had painted his famous *Nude Descending a Staircase*, so Rosie did a painting of a *Man Ascending a Staircase*. It was Juan on the wide staircase at the Alcazar, walking out of her life. Scattered on the stairs were fractured guitars and bleeding flowers, torn sheets of music and melting clown faces.

Señora Calderón arrived a few days later to see how the work was coming for the exhibit. Rosie was not sure how the agent would like this new turn her work had taken. But somehow, she didn't care anymore. Whatever Calderón had to say was unimportant. Only the art mattered. She was putting down what she knew she must. They were like angry demons that emptied out into colors and shapes on the canvasses. She could not paint enough to keep up with their increasing demands.

Señora Calderón studied each painting quietly, standing back, closing her steely grey eyes for a brief second, then resuming her study. She lined them up against the narrow ledge in almost the exact order in which Rosie had painted them. "How did you know the chronological order of my work, Señora Calderón?"

"When you have dealt in art as long as I have, you will know. You already have more than enough for the exhibit. And still you paint?"

"I paint because I must, not for the exhibit. You will have a great number to choose from."

"If they are all like these last ten, I shall make room for them all."

"Do you like them, then?"

"I am your agent, not your critic. Your work will sell. That is all I am concerned with. If you did not paint what would sell, I wouldn't bother with you. But you want an opinion, so I will tell you what has happened to your work since I first saw it. You have had a deep, devastating experience, and you have put it all into your work. Consider yourself lucky to be an artist, because a normal person exhibiting these emotions would be locked up. Continue to paint. I cannot deal with emotional upheavals and breakdowns. An artist gives the emotions to his work and, in most cases, saves his sanity. Poor van Gogh did not have enough canvasses to fill, and he was lost."

"But do artists continue to work well when they are happy, Señora Calderón? Must I always be in the throes of misery to create?" Rosie tried to look at her paintings as an outsider, and they were decidedly powerful, emotional statements.

"All your emotions, happy or sad, will show up in your work," she said confidently. "The work will always be touched with genius, but the styles may change according to your mood. Picasso went through many phases. I shall take all these back to Madrid with me to have them framed. Any that you do in the next two weeks before the opening, take them to my framer here each day so that they will be ready to hang. By the way, the Countess will be giving you a reception the night of your opening. All the celebrities in town will be there. She tells me you see the matador, Manuel Herrera. He receives excellent press coverage— even better than your ex-boyfriend Arévalo, though he used to bring out the paparrazzi when he was having his affair with that terrible British actress, Jane something-or-other."

"Jane Sidney," Rosie offered reluctantly.

"Sidney, yes. Well, I spoke to Manuel's manager and he said Manuel was scheduled to fight in Barcelona the day of your opening, and he was very reluctant to contact his client about any planned publicity romance. Spanish men tend to have an aversion to that sort of thing. Most difficult for us to work with. I much prefer Americans or Frenchmen. But he did contact Manuel for me. He owes me several favors and was quite surprised to find that Manuel was anxious to attend your opening and would be your escort if you wished. Evidently he was quite impressed with your work, for his manager said that must be understood. So it is very good for us. He will fly in from Barcelona after the bullfight and join you at your opening. His arrival will cause a great stir, especially when it is known that it is out of appreciation for your work, and not especially romance that has brought him in from Barcelona."

Rosie wondered at the complexity of these psychological press maneuverings. "What you do is quite an art in itself," she commented.

Señora Calderón managed a thin smile. "One does not realize what goes on behind the scenes. Now, one more thing. The Marqués de Arévalo will be at your opening, too, I imagine, because of the, uh, family connections? I called his manager and he confirmed that Arévalo would be in Madrid Saturday night for a special flamenco recital, but he could not confirm whether or not he would come to your opening on Sunday."

"I don't know if he will be there," said Rosie uneasily. "He might, for the family's sake. We really are not on very good terms."

"But you will be attending *his* concert, won't you?"

"I ... I don't know."

Chapter Twenty

JUAN HAD CALLED several times, each time asking to speak to Rosie, but she continued to refuse. He told his mother that he had reserved seats for them all at the theatre and rooms for them at the Palace Hotel. Rosie learned that she was included in his plans and would have turned them all down but that she had to be in Madrid anyway, and it would save money to share a room with Señora Gómez.

For the family's sake, she promised to attend the performance. It would have been rude to do otherwise. Besides, she could not let her personal feelings get in the way of appreciation for Juan's music. He was still the finest flamenco guitarist in Spain, and she had collected all his records even before she had met him.

In the back of her mind she held a slender thread of hope that the guitar recital would somehow bring them back together. Though her work had gone well over the past few weeks, her longings for Juan had become nearly unbearable. She had even resolved that the next time he called, she would speak to him.

But the day arrived that they were all to fly to Madrid, he had called again that morning to reconfirm all the plans, but this time he did not ask for Rosie.

Rafaela and Danny chatted gaily in the airplane seats across from her and the Señora. They were filled with anticipation and excitement. Rosie envied them. How much easier it was to be on the periphery of an event, than deep inside it. "*Mi* Rosa," said the Señora, "You look so very serious. You should be happy about your exhibit! This is what you have wanted all your life."

169

"To tell you the truth, I'm frightened to death."

"But of what can you be frightened? Señora Calderón has seen to everything."

"I have butterflies fluttering in the pit of my stomach. What if nobody likes my paintings? I will have to stand there and listen to people talk about my work. I remember my exhibits in Kansas that were such disasters. People talk about your paintings as though they were separate from you. They don't understand that it is *you* they criticize, not the painting."

Señora Gómez patted her hand reassuringly. "Rosa, inside your heart, you know your paintings are good, no?"

Rosie nodded.

"Then, that is all that matters. You must be strong. But I know that they will love your art. How can they not love what is so beautiful?"

Rosie wished she had the same confidence. But it was not just the exhibit that troubled her. What if Juan did not want her? That would be worse than having the exhibit fail. She longed to confide in Señora Gómez, but she dared not. Worst of all seemed to be the prospect of having someone say knowingly, "You see, I told you so."

The Palace Hotel was the most elegant place Rosie had ever seen. Juan had reserved adjoining rooms for them that overlooked a huge plaza below. The larger of the rooms was more like a suite. At one end was a raised platform with two double beds and at the other were velvet armchairs and a couch placed around a marble coffee table with a huge dome overhead. Danny walked through the room and whistled. Then he burst into laughter. "Rafaela, come here. Listen." He whistled again. The dome was so constructed that there was a slight echo. "Now this is one classy room!"

Juan had seen that each room had a large basket of fresh fruit. Soft drinks and liquor were in small refrigerators, and there was a beautiful flower arrangement on the table.

Señora Gómez was beside herself. She crossed the large room, touched the fine furniture reverently. "Mamá is finally a marquesa," Rafaela whispered to Rosie. "She always

said that was not what she wanted, but I think she would
have loved it anyway. Look at the way her eyes light up."

Juan telephoned to say that he would be unable to see
them until after the recital, but that he wanted them to come
backstage afterwards. "He asked if you would be coming,
Rosa," said the Señora, "and he seemed pleased to hear that
you were."

Rosie could feel her hands tremble, but tried not to show
how excited she was.

There were several hours to kill before the performance.
Señora Gómez wanted to take a nap, so Rosie, Danny and
Rafaela went out for a walk. Rosie wanted to go back to
the Prado Museum, but Danny convinced her that there
wasn't enough time.

It was a sunny afternoon, but most of the shops, in
Spanish tradition, were closed until 5:00 P.M. so there was
not much to do but walk. In a charming little plaza that had
a statue of Cervantes there was a newsstand with international publications, including a Herald Tribune. Since
it was a pleasant day, they found a park bench under the
statue and poured through, each taking a section. Rafaela
was practicing her English on the society page, figuring it
would be the easiest to understand. "Oh, look, here is a
picture of Jane Sidney."

Even the sound of her name made Rosie's skin crawl,
but Rafaela knew nothing about the scene that had taken
place that morning in Cordoba.

"Isn't that the actress we saw in Seville?" Danny asked.
"Read what it says, hon."

"There are words I'm not sure of," she apologized. "*Mi
amor*, you read it."

Rosie watched Danny's face turn scarlet. "Oh, it's just
something about some movie she's in," he said quickly and
handed the paper back to Rafaela.

"Well, what does it say?" asked Rafaela.

Rosie knew by Danny's expression that there was something more. Quietly she took the newspaper from Rafaela.
"Here, I'll read it for you."

Even the newsprint face staring up at her with the heavily

mascaraed eyes and white skin enraged Rosie, but not as much as when she read: "'British star Jane Sidney, seen lunching at Trader Vic's with producer Hal Van Neft, says she is returning to Spain at the end of the week to attend a guitar recital in Madrid. The on-again-off-again stormy romance between Sidney and flamenco guitarist Juan de Arévalo seems to be 'on again.' They were seen together at their favorite corner table at Tour d'Argent in Paris where Arévalo was performing on French TV. Friends close to the actress say marriage plans may be in the offing.'"

The last sentence almost did not come out, for Rosie felt herself grow faint as she said the words. How could he marry that horrible woman? It made a mockery of everything beautiful the two of them had shared. She saw the fiery-haired woman again luxuriating on Juan's satin sheets on the high Spanish bed, that affected shrill voice calling herself the Marquesa de Arévalo.

Rosie stood up and began walking aimlessly down the street. Never had she felt so bewildered or distraught. It was as though an arrow had been shot through her heart. She hardly knew how she would make it through the day, much less through the weekend. How could she ever go to the concert?

"Rosie, it couldn't be true. You know how those gossip columnists are. She probably paid them to print that for publicity. You said yourself that those things are all manipulated by managers and agents. Look at the coverage Señora Calderón has gotten for you in the Madrid newspapers already. You read those clippings she sent over to the hotel. All that business about you and Manuel Herrera. You and I know it's a lot of bunk just to get people to your opening. How can you believe this stuff about Jane Sidney?"

As much as she would have liked to believe what her brother said, as much sense as it made, Rosie could not rid herself of the loathsome image of Jane Sidney in Juan's bedroom, her flaunting act in the pink silk pantsuit. If Jane were at the recital tonight, then she would know for sure that the article had been correct.

*   *   *

At the last minute, Rosie tried to fake a headache to stay away from the theater, but Danny quickly saw through it and bolstered her up. "You have got to go. Do you know how Señora Gómez will feel if you don't? Are you such a coward that a silly article will make you miss hearing the music of a man you have idolized for years? Forget the way you feel about him."

Juan had sent a chauffeured limousine for them. All the way to the theater, Rosie tried to remain calm, and pretended to be as enthusiastic as Rafaela and Señora Gómez. She must not spoil their enjoyment.

It was a shock to see Juan's photograph on the cover program. She had almost forgotten that his handsome, aristocratic face with the deep-set dark eyes she loved belonged to the public. She scanned the program to see what he would play. There was the *Canción Triste* by Calleja that she loved; two compositions by Fernando Sors; *seguidillas*, the passionate gypsy love songs; a *soleare*, the Andalusian cry of loneliness and what she was searching for, at the very end of the program, *Romance de Amor*. Was it there for her? Or for Jane Sidney?

Rosie had watched the audience carefully, but even as the house lights were dimming, she had not seen Jane Sidney arrive. Suddenly, there was a general murmuring in the audience. Of course, Jane Sidney would wait to make her entrance. In a full length mink coat that brushed the floor, she swept in, accompanied by two men in tuxedos.

Rosie braced herself for the performance, determined to enjoy it in spite of the crushed, defeated heart that pounded within her.

There was no orchestra. This was to be a solo performance of Juan and his guitar. A chair was placed center stage as the curtain rose. Juan walked in with his guitar and bowed slightly to the audience, an air of solemnity that she had never seen on him before. The audience applauded wildly to see him, and she found herself caught up in it like the rest of them. Was this the same man she had lain so intimately with, who had wrapped his strong arms around her and spoken of love?

How alone he seemed there on the large stage, in his black tuxedo, the white shirt accenting his tan face and thick black hair. Even from the distance, she could see the dark luminosity of his large eyes.

The audience grew hushed. There was a cough. Someone cleared his throat. Juan waited until there was perfect silence, then began.

Rosie felt shivers down her back. The impact of his playing was like nothing she had ever experienced before. In a way, it was more intimate than his lovemaking. Whatever touched her was reaching everyone else in the large concert hall.

She was glad she had come. Whatever had become of their relationship would never affect her love of his music, and knowing that, she let herself be transported by the pleading strains of the flamenco chords. She understood now how the guitar carried the soul of the Spanish people in its depths. She looked at his mother sitting next to her. Tears ran down her face. Rosie reached over and held her hand. A silent understanding passed between the two women as they listened to the man who held their very souls in his hands.

During the brief intermission, Rosie stood in the lobby chatting with the Countess. "My, wasn't he marvelous? I've heard him dozens of times, of course. Here and in London and Paris, but tonight, I think he's absolutely the best. Something about playing in your own country, don't you think, dear?"

"Yes, of course," said Rosie.

"And you must be so excited about *your* day tomorrow. I have everything planned for the party afterward. You're my special little project, you know. After all, it was I who discovered you."

Rosie barely heard what the Countess said for she saw Jane Sidney swooping toward her, the two tuxedoed gentlemen like comical penguins trailing after her. "My darling,

Rose, it's been ages, hasn't it?" She kissed Rosie on both
cheeks as Rosie stood stiffly, hatred blazing from her eyes.

"Well, we simply *must* talk. I promised Juan I would.
You know how he is," she sighed dramatically.

"I don't believe we have anything to say to each other,"
said Rosie coldly.

"Oh, but we *do*, dearest. But this is so *public*, you
know?"

"Don't mind me," said the Countess, waving her blue
tipped fingers.

Rosie took a deep breath. "Miss Sidney, spare yourself
the effort."

The lights dimmed on and off in signal that the recital
was to begin again.

"Perhaps tomorrow night at the Countess's, darling, we
can have our little heart to heart," Jane called after her with
a cheery smile.

"When hell freezes over," muttered Rosie under her
breath. If Juan wanted to tell her that he was marrying Jane,
he could have the guts to tell her himself.

She wondered how she could possibly enjoy the re-
mainder of the concert after the run-in with Jane, but it was
only minutes before the music overcame her. Just before
his final piece, Juan looked out into the audience, as though
searching for a face. He stared in her direction, his eyes
eloquent. For a fleeting moment, Rosie's hopes rose. Was
he trying to signal her? With all her heart, she tried to reach
him with the sheer force of her feelings.

He began to play *Romance de Amor*. Even the afternoon
she had heard it in his *palacio*, it had not been as beautiful.
Each note brought back a scene of their love. She watched
his fingers strum the intricate chords and remembered what
he had done to her own body, how he had made it sing as
eloquently as his guitar. Every tear she had shed thinking
of him became part of the music, the terrible longing, the
pain and tenderness of their passion.

There was a standing ovation as he closed and he played
several encores. She thought the audience would never let

him finish, but finally he bowed and left the stage for the last time.

The crowd backstage was thick. She could see Juan standing taller than the others. He was smiling, politely accepting the congratulations on a fine performance. Suddenly she saw him look through the people at her. Their eyes caught and held. Leaving the others in mid-sentence, he made his way through the crowd toward her.

Her heart was pounding wildly. He hugged his mother, kissed Rafaela, hoped they enjoyed the performance, was glad Danny had come ... but he was looking at Rosie. Her turn was coming. What would he say?

He grabbed her hand and held it in both of his. "I was hoping you'd come, Rosa." Why didn't he take her in his arms? She wanted him so much.

"It ... it was a wonderful recital," she managed.

"I have reserved a table at Horcher's for all of us. You will come, won't you?"

"Why I ..."

Before she could speak, Jane Sidney had made her presence loudly known. "It's impossible to get to you, darling," she sighed dramatically. "These wild throngs of stuffy people. Why must there always be so many people backstage?"

"Did you talk to Rosa?" he asked Jane anxiously.

"There wasn't time, love. But I *will*. Is it Horcher's tonight as usual?"

That was all Rosie needed to hear. It was hard enough standing there between Juan and Jane. She could not sit and watch the rest of the evening while the two of them held hands in the restaurant and announced their engagement and talked about *their* wedding plans.

She excused herself quickly. "I don't feel well. I'm going back to the hotel," she mumbled and grabbed a taxi at the curb.

She rushed up to the hotel suite and threw herself across the bed. The phone rang several minutes after she arrived, but she did not answer it. It rang again and again at intervals of about ten minutes. Finally, she picked up the receiver.

"Rosie, hi, what happened to you?" It was Danny. She felt a disappointment that it was not Juan. She had dared to hope.

"I didn't feel well, so I came back here."

"Juan has been trying to call you. He asked me to try for awhile 'cause he had to be with his guests. He was worried about you. Why don't you get yourself together and get a cab. We're all at this fantastic restaurant."

"No, I'm not hungry."

"Rosie!"

"I'm *not*, Danny. I just want to rest."

"Are you sure it's not Jane Sidney?"

"No," Rosie lied.

"All right then," he seemed willing to take her at her word. "Look, get some rest. You have a big day tomorrow. I'll explain to everyone."

Rosie cried for a long time. She did not have her canvasses now to fill with her grief, only a pillow. She was still awake when she heard the others come in, tiptoeing so they wouldn't wake her.

But she did not sleep well that night. How ironic, it seemed to her, that at the moment of her biggest success professionally, she would experience simultaneously the greatest failure in her personal life.

She had only herself to blame for losing Juan, and the exhibit tomorrow was the very reason. A strangling thought crossed her mind that caused her to tremble with fear. What if the exhibit, too, was a failure?

Chapter Twenty-one

JUAN WAS COMING by to take them all to lunch, but Rosie had to meet Señora Calderón at the gallery early in the morning and go over the placement of the paintings.

Rafaela told her briefly about their evening at Horcher's as she downed a quick cup of room service coffee. "You should have seen my mother's face when he introduced her to everyone as his mother. Do you remember in Seville, he was very kind but never did he actually call her his mother, or me his sister. But last night, he told us that he had never publicly said anything because he was afraid for our feelings. As for him, he was very proud to be her son and would like it to be finally in the open. He had her sit next to him at the table and treated her, well, like a marquesa. It was so very beautiful to see, Rosa. I wish you had been there. He mentioned several times to me that he wished you were there."

"What about Jane Sidney. Where did she sit?"

"Jane Sidney? She was at another table entirely. Rosie, I cannot believe what was in the newspapers. He barely spoke to her last night."

Rosie did not have time to question Rafaela further, but she wondered if she hadn't been too quick to think the worst. How was it the paper reported that he had been seen with Jane in Paris. Surely that wasn't fiction, and why had she wanted to talk?

There were a million details to attend to at the gallery. It had never occurred to her before that certain paintings could be shown to better advantage when placed next to others. In general, she was pleased with the gallery. The lighting was excellent, and the walls and carpet were a soft grey that made the intense colors of her compositions come alive.

Señora Calderón, once she was satisfied with the exhibit, dragged Rosie off for a final fitting of the gown she had ordered for her. She had been skeptical about letting Señora Calderón choose a dress for her without even seeing herself in it, but it had been another of the details that Rosie had left to the agent's discretion. She had no idea what was proper to wear at one's own gallery opening.

When Rosie first saw the black silk with the scalloped hem, she thought it looked very severe, but once she had it on, she realized that the simple cut accentuated her soft curves. It was discreet, but cut quite low, showing the white roundness of her small breasts.

Señora Calderón loaned her a long strand of pearls to complete the outfit. "I've read that pearls are coming back and I've had these for years. They're real. Bought them in the Orient. Basic black and pearls. Somehow it always works. I would have picked something more flamboyant for you, but your work is so highly charged, I thought it would be better to dress you in a contrasting color. Now, I have a 4:00 P.M. appointment for you at the Palace Hotel hairdresser. There's a marvelous Frenchman there. The French are the only ones who can do hair. Remember that, wherever you are, find a Frenchman. He's going to give you something fluffy to counteract the dress. Wear a bright lipstick, otherwise you'll fade away."

"Señora Calderón," she said nervously. "Do you think the critics will like my work?"

"Of course, they will. I've paid them to like it. We're here to *sell* paintings, not create art history. Just hope people *buy* the paintings. Now get yourself a taxi and get back to the hotel for your hair appointment. I will see you at the gallery promptly at seven. The others will begin arriving at eight, though these blasted celebrities are always late."

The French hairdresser was a nervous little man who spoke in a heavy accent. He was not happy with her fingernails or her makeup, and before she left the salon, she had been metamorphosed. An unfamiliar face stared back at her in the mirror, but she was too nervous to protest.

Danny whistled when she walked into the hotel suite. "Look at her, will you! Rosie, they've really made you *look* like somebody famous. I could take you back to Wichita and people you grew up with wouldn't recognize you."

"When are you all arriving there tonight?" she asked nervously.

"Juan said he would be here with the limo at eight. Can't you come with us?" asked Rafaela.

"Señora Calderón wants me there early, though heaven only knows what I'll do while I'm waiting. I'm shaken up as it is."

Calderón gave Rosie two shots of brandy to calm her nerves. "But no more of that. I once had an artist too drunk to socialize with the patrons. It's bad business. You must constantly wear a smile and be polite no matter what stupid things people say about your work. An artist's presence gives people confidence to buy."

Surprisingly, in spite of his bullfight in Barcelona, Manuel Herrera arrived before anyone. She was so glad to see a friendly face—someone who knew her well enough that she did not have to play a role—that she hugged him tightly to her. "I'm so glad you're here; I've been dying."

"I know how you feel. It is always that way for me when I first see the bull. I showered at the bullring and had my driver take me straight to the Barcelona airport. All the shuttle flights were full of weekend traffic, but one of my fans stepped aside to give me his seat. So you see, it is not always bad to be famous, eh? My God, Rosa. Look at this work!"

He was the first one outside the immediate family, Señora Calderón and the gallery owner, who had seen her work set up in the exhibit. It was the greatest boost of confidence she could have received.

"I saw only this one," he pointed to her painting of Manolete's former assistant. "But they are, every one, magnificent. I want to be your first patron. Calderón, come here. I want to buy this painting. I was there the day she painted it!" he said with pride.

Señora Calderón gave Rosie a small smile. She was pleased to be able to tell people that Manuel Herrera had just bought a painting.

He slipped his arm around her. "And how beautiful you look tonight, the contrast of the black silk next to your silky white skin, your golden hair and emerald eyes . . ." He brushed her lips lightly with a kiss and, as he did, Rosie saw beyond him Juan de Arévalo walk through the door.

Chapter Twenty-two

Juan was with the family, but Rosie could see he was holding back. She wanted to break away from Manuel and rush into his arms. But the others were upon her, talking excitedly. Juan came up to them more slowly. "Congratulations, Rosa."

She was flushed and was unable to speak.

"And congratulations to you too, Manuel. I heard you won two ears and a tail this afternoon."

Rosie suddenly understood why Juan was acting so coldly formal. Manuel Herrera's arm was still tightly around her waist. If only she could break loose without seeming rude.

But Señora Calderón materialized with a photographer in tow. "I want a picture of the two of you beside the painting he just bought. There, that's right. No, move to the left a little so we can see the painting. I'm not selling love, I'm selling paintings."

The flash camera blinded Rosie for a moment, and when she blinked her way clear, Juan was across the room, looking at the exhibit. Calderón was introducing her to people on one side and Manuel was introducing her on the other. She felt like a juggler, smiling to one side, trying to remember what someone said on the other, trying to keep track of where Juan was in the room.

He must know by these paintings how much I love him. If I cannot tell him, they must tell him for me. All my work is infused with love of him. He cannot fail to see it.

She noticed that he was not going quickly through the room, but stopping for some time in front of each canvas, standing back, studying, going closer up, then moving back again. She remembered how he had behaved that first day she had seen him in the Prado. Once she thought she caught his eye, but it was fleeting. Someone else stepped into her view and began talking at a rapid pace.

Rafaela wedged into the crowd surrounding her for a moment and caught her ear. "Everyone is in love with your paintings, Rosa. I have been around the room listening."

"Have you talked to Juan; what does he think?"

"He is very mysterious. He won't say a thing, but he goes very slowly. Perhaps he is embarrassed to see what they are about."

Just when she felt she could not bear to stand in her high heels another moment and stretch her face into another smile, a hand grabbed hers and pulled her away from Manuel. She looked up with surprise and saw that it was Jane Sidney.

"Come on, darling, I have to talk to you. Juan has threatened to strangle me or commit some equally odious crime if I don't have a word with you this very minute."

Señora Calderón was there quickly to intercept.

"Calderón, my precious, I'm just taking your star attraction out to the little girl's room for a moment. The matador will keep the masses entertained while she is gone. This is a matter of life or death—mine."

How strange being grateful to a woman you loathe, thought Rosie, but she was glad to have an excuse to leave, if only for a few moments. They found an empty office toward the back of the gallery, and both women kicked off their shoes and massaged their feet before a word was spoken. It was a funny scene and Rosie found herself laughing in spite of herself.

"Gawd, the shoes this year are enough to make a person a cripple."

"What did you want to talk to me about?" Rosie decided to get to the point.

Rosie saw a different expression cross the face of the actress, one she had not seen before. It was as though it were finally stripped of pretentions and heavy makeup. "It's about that stupid scene I pulled at Arévalo's in Cordoba. I'm on so much, you know, in front of the camera, that sometimes I get carried away with myself. I didn't realize until Juan told me in Paris that you two were actually getting married. I was just throwing words around. He and I were never serious . . . at least *he* wasn't." There was a profound sadness in the actress's wide eyes that went beyond the stage. "I did care more for him than I let on. He didn't know it. I'm a pretty good actress at that. When I saw you two together at the *feria* in Seville, I knew he was in love for the first time in his life and it made me angry and jealous. I haven't told Juan any of this, mind you. I just told him I was having a little fun that morning in Cordoba. He found out I was in Paris and took me to lunch, made me promise to straighten things out with you. So there you are, luv. True confessions. Can we be friends, now?"

"Sure," said Rosie warmly. She felt a little sorry for the glamorous star. In spite of her fame and fortune, there were still things in life beyond her reach.

"Well, let's get these damn shoes back on and get our smiles in place. Our public is waiting," Jane laughed. Rosie saw that her actress's mask was also back in place.

The thick crowd was still clamoring around Manuel Herrera and, before Calderón could whisk her back into the center of it, she surveyed the room for Juan. He was standing not far away, watching her.

"Juan—Jane told me . . ."

He came toward her and she felt her knees go weak, just as they always did in his commanding presence. "Was that why you refused to come last night, or was it Manuel? Are you seeing Manuel again?"

"How many times do I have to tell you that there is nothing between me and Manuel except friendship!"

"A man flies in from Barcelona an hour after his bullfight for nothing? So he bought one of your paintings. And *this* dress too?" He touched the silk on her shoulder and she shuddered, flushing deep scarlet.

Juan's dark eyes were blazing with molten heat. "I see

clearly what you have done, Rosa. You have used me, all the love I felt for you, and have smeared your canvasses with it. Did you take it so lightly that you could put it on public display, sell it to the highest bidder, capitalize on our relationship. What will the next exhibit be about? Shall I guess? Will those canvasses be filled with bullfighters?"

He turned away with disgust and began to walk toward the door.

Rosie forgot who and where she was. Her only thought was getting Juan back. She could not let him leave her, not again.

Calderón was coming toward her. "Come on, dear. Get your coat. We're all ready to go back to the Palace Hotel for the Countess's party in your honor."

Rosie ignored her and flew out the door coatless after Juan. She caught up with him just as he was about to get into a taxi and dug her fingers into his arm. "Juan—you don't understand. Please don't run off like this."

He took her fingers off his arm one by one and said coldly, "It's not polite to leave your guests." He got into the taxi, but before he could close the door, she jumped in beside him.

"I don't care about them. You are the only thing I care about in the whole world, Juan. Don't you understand? Those paintings, they were all *my* love for you. All the agony and pain I've felt these months, wanting you every minute. The only place I could express it was in my work. An artist must paint what is burning inside. Didn't Goya cover his canvasses with portraits of his mistress, the Duchess of Alba? You want to make it seem like cheap commercialism; that is Señora Calderón's job. It's not the paintings and the exhibit. But I don't see you playing your guitar in a closet all by yourself."

She could see by his eyes that he had softened. He told the driver to take them to the Palace Hotel. He put his arms around her. Their lips found each other and, in the moments that followed, all the past tribulations melted away.

"Rosa, I did see all that in the paintings. And I hoped it was the love you felt for me. Last night at the recital, knowing you were in the audience made a difference in my playing. I saw your face as I played, and sounds came out of the guitar that surprised me. You and I need each other; we need the inspiration of our love. I did not really see it until tonight at your exhibit. Before, I had only seen your sketches, a few watercolors. I could not understand the great genius that lay hidden inside you, waiting to be released. It was impossible for me, with my ego and my success as a musician, to see how important your art was too. We *must* be together, Rosa. It is fated. Neither one of us would be complete with the other."

As they stepped out of the taxi, cameras flashed again in their faces and, through the lights, Rosie was shocked to see that Señora Calderón had beaten them to the hotel.

"Thank heaven," Señora Calderón sighed. "I was afraid for a moment you had run out. But I was sure you had too much sense for that. Hello, Juan. Could you two stand over there just a minute so the photographers can get a better angle. That's it. Oh, a kiss, good. Now, come along. The Countess has the champagne on ice."

Juan and Rosie looked at each other and grinned. "We will have a whole lifetime of this," he whispered.

"Then a few minutes alone won't matter at this juncture, would it?"

"Not at all," his dark eyes sparkled.

"Calderón, we'll be there shortly. Don't get that morose expression. You know a slightly late entrance is good theater. Have the photographers ready, and tell the press we are going to make an important announcement. No one will dare leave until we arrive."

Señora Calderón threw up her hands. "You're right, you're right. Come on," she said to the photographers, dragging them off through the lobby.

Juan and Rosie ran to the elevator and slipped into his room.

"Oh, Juan, this is crazy. We haven't much time."

"Not right now, perhaps, Rosa," he said as he drew her close, "but we will have the whole rest of our lives."